Ardent Apparitions

Also by Ellen Fitzgerald

The Damsels from Derbyshire

Ardent Apparitions

Ellen Fitzgerald

Walker and Company
New York

First published in the United States of America in 1992 by
Walker Publishing Company, Inc.

Published simultaneously in Canada by Thomas Allen & Son
Canada, Limited, Markham, Ontario

Library of Congress Cataloging-in-Publication Data
Fitzgerald, Ellen.
Ardent apparitions / Ellen Fitzgerald
p.   cm.
ISBN 0-8027-1209-6 (cloth)
I. Title.
PS3569.T455A89   1992
813'.54—dc20   92-4656
CIP

Printed in the United States of America

2   4   6   8   10   9   7   5   3   1

Ardent Apparitions

=== 1 ===

"BURIED TREASURE OR no buried treasure, it is entirely incredible, amazing, stupefying and— I vow, I have run out of words, Arabella." Miss Clemency Beresford, her blue eyes dark with indignation and amazement, regarded her best friend incredulously. "Do you believe in this so-called treasure?"

"How am I to believe or not believe in it?" Lady Arabella Arden demanded, gazing indignantly at Clemency. "Actually, I do not think I do believe in it. I am of the opinion that it is Papa's way of trying to make me feel better for barring my way to Paris—sending me off to this moldering castle and to a great-great-aunt of whom I have never heard!" She paused, adding, "Well, actually, I have heard of her; it was years and years ago. She is a relation of my mother, and I expect that is why she is so rarely mentioned. Papa does not like to talk of her family—it casts him into the dismals."

"Great-great," Clemency mused. "That would mean that she is your great-grandmother's sister. My gracious, she must be a hundred and ten!"

"Her youngest sister," Arabella amplified with a roll of her much-praised eyes—compared by one of her suitors to the ocean on certain stormy days when its waters were a dark green.

"How young can she be?" Clemency asked. "If she is your great-great-aunt?"

"I did not say she was young. I said she was the youn-

1

gest sister of my great-grandmother. She is, I believe, close on ninety and undoubtedly in her dotage." Arabella's eyes grew even stormier. "And I am to be incarcerated in her moldy castle, which is two hundred miles from London."

"I thought it was one hundred and ninety-nine," Clemency said.

"You'd quibble for a mile?" Arabella demanded crossly.

"Of course not. I am sorry." Clemency blushed. "But why did you not point out to your papa that we would be glad to shelter you until he returns from France?"

"I did point it out, several times, but my aunt Margaret—whom I shall never forgive if I live to be a hundred—said that I am looking a bit peaked and that, in her estimation, I need a rest from the rigors of town life! Oh!" Arabella rose and took a turn around the chamber. "I could kill her!"

"That would avail you nothing and you would either be hanged or transported. I have an uncle who is in the administration of New South Wales, and he loathes the place even though he is living in comfort—compared to what the prisoners must endure."

"Silly!" Arabella directed a caustic glance at her friend. "I did not literally mean I could kill her. I just think she is far too interfering! She is not my mother, after all."

"Well," Clemency said thoughtfully, "since your mother died only hours after you were born, and since your aunt has been living with you for so many years, I expect she feels as if she were your mother. You ought to be glad your papa did not marry again. I am sure your aunt is preferable to a stepmother. Rosalie Bennington absolutely loathes her father's new wife."

"Drat Rosalie Bennington. I want to stay with you."

"And we want you to come. You do not look at all 'wasted by the rigors of town life,' as your aunt insists."

"They do not trust me," Arabella said angrily. "And it is not my fault that Sir Julian Foxworthy wrote a sonnet to my 'burnished beauty,' by which I hope he meant my hair and not my complexion."

"Of course he meant your hair, my dear. It is a lovely color, red in some lights and—"

"Brown in others," Arabella said, pouting.

"It could never be adjudged plain brown, Arabella. It is all shades. Most unusual, Mama says."

"I would rather have your blond hair, or as Shakespeare said about Portia, your 'sunny locks.' "

"He also compared them to golden fleece, if you will remember." Clemency grimaced. "Golden or not—that line always reminds me of a sheep. If my hair were curlier, but I am certainly glad it is not. Perhaps if I had Mama speak to your papa. She can be very persuasive."

"Papa might have listened had not Carola Lyndhurst eloped with that Captain of the Life Guards. Because I had a very slight acquaintance with Carola, he and my aunt appear to believe me infected with a similar desire; even though I have repeatedly assured them that there is no one with whom I want to elope! Unfortunately, my father's departure for France fits in with my aunt's plans to go to Scotland and be present at the lying-in of her daughter, whom she never sees unless she is in a delicate condition. Rosalie lives in the Highlands."

"Poor Carola." Clemency sighed. "I wonder how she is faring."

"I, too, even though she has ruined my life and possibly her own."

"You are exaggerating, Arabella. Charlie Anstruthers is very well-connected even if he doesn't have a feather to fly with. Moreover, he looks very handsome in his uniform. I shouldn't have minded eloping with him were it not for my lovely Lord Mapleton."

This conversation was very much in Arabella's mind as, with her aunt and their two abigails, they penetrated into the vast loneliness that was Yorkshire, under a sky whose cerulean blue was temporarily blotted out by the swift gathering of great gray clouds.

Staring out at them, Arabella's depression increased. Her aunt seemed similarly cast down. Indeed, much to

3

Arabella's relief, she had ceased to extol the beauty of the surrounding countryside. Mighty castles crowned distant hills, but there was a singular paucity of houses, and vast stretches of moorland that, though covered with summer's panoply of short, verdant grass, curling fronds of young bracken, and the brilliant yellow of sweet-smelling, honey-laden gorse blooms contrasting so strikingly with their somber foliage, still appeared extremely lonely. It seemed to Arabella that it had taken days and days to reach Yorkshire. Though they had stayed at various inns along the road, by now Arabella was of the opinion, shared by her aunt, that she could not endure the motion of the swaying coach another hour—much less a day! Worse yet, Meg, her abigail, had been in a most depressed mood, augmented by that same motion to the point that they had needed to stop several times along the road to accommodate her—something that appeared to amuse Rose, Lady Margaret's abigail, which in turn angered Meg. Though neither girl made any comments, the atmosphere in the coach was heavy with a repressed annoyance that was very difficult to ignore. Indeed, Arabella was of the opinion that if they did not soon reach their destination, she would give them both a tongue-lashing they would not soon forget—which, of course, would only make matters worse!

Then, on passing through a village, they suddenly started up a steep hill. Gazing out her window, Arabella saw another castle at its crest, and Lady Margaret, leaning forward to ask the coachman where they were headed, learned that finally they were nearing their destination!

From this distance, the castle appeared to be singularly massive. On either side of frowning battlements rose a tall tower, and Arabella guessed that there might be other towers hidden in the trees that flanked it. There was also a bridge that, she was sure, must span a moat. Before she could draw any more conclusions, they rounded a bend in the road and the castle was momentarily lost to view.

Despite her resentment at being "prisoned" in this

mighty edifice, Arabella found herself oddly excited. The gothic novels she and Clemency read so avidly had contained descriptions of just such castles and, furthermore, this one appeared to be in extremely good condition. That was surprising for, to her certain knowledge, it dated back to the fifteenth century and rose on the grounds of an even earlier castle built at the time of Richard I. The present building had been erected shortly after Henry V ascended the throne—in 1417, to be exact. In common with Richard I, his reign had lasted a scant ten years, she remembered. Though their lives had been brief, both had been responsible for numerous deaths in such far-flung places as Jerusalem, and also in France. She shivered. Even though large numbers of the slain had been enemies, she found herself unwilling to dwell upon the so-called glory attendant on the actions of those two monarchs.

These melancholy thoughts were suddenly dispersed by the sight of a man on horseback galloping past her window. She had a brief glimpse of a merry smile, dark flashing eyes, and, much to her surprise, long dark hair! She had an impression that he was also clad in dark garments and that they were not quite the usual style. She looked out of the window, hoping to see him again, but just then the coach rounded another bend and they were once more in sight of the castle.

It was, Arabella saw, indeed in an excellent state of preservation—looking at those solid walls, one would never guess that it was nearly four hundred years old! Had she been in a mood to be excited about being shut in a lonely edifice miles from the nearest town, she might have been pleased at staying in this hoary structure. She had read a great many gothic novels in which a castle was prominently featured and always haunted. She adored tales of ghost-ridden castles, a predilection her father regretted.

"There are no such things as ghosts, Arabella. They arise out of unhealthy imaginations and diseased brains and, in my opinion, all these so-called 'gothic' novels you and your friends devour should be burned in one large pyre along with . . ."

He had not finished his sentence but Arabella guessed that he had intended to say "along with their authors" before thinking better of it. Furthermore, that statement, summarily dismissing the numerous shades said to frequent castles belonging to various of his friends, had both irked and disappointed her.

Lord Dartmoor was extremely intelligent and was known to have been an exceptionally brilliant scholar at Oxford. Indeed, his tutor had urged him to remain and become a Fellow of his college. This his family responsibilities precluded, however, as Fellows were required to be celibate and he was the last of his line. Consequently, given these same intellectual attainments, argument was futile and she had perforce to believe him. Still, even though the "enlightened mind" had to reject them, she had been unable to put aside her "haunted" novels in favor of Jane Austen and Walter Scott and other celebrated authors currently residing in England. Indeed, hidden under two layers of garments in her portmanteau were the last volume of *The Demon of Sicily,* three volumes of *The Mysterious Hand,* and four volumes of *The Grey Nun,* a work Clemency had recommended highly, all of which made the castle looming before her more acceptable than it had been when only a subject of tears and defiance.

The way to the castle was uphill, and the horses' pace was necessarily slow as they strained to ascend it. Arabella, looking out of her window, was surprised at the steepness of the curving road behind her. Then that emotion gave way to shock as, once more, she spied a horseman coming around a bend. It was the same man she had seen earlier, she realized. She recognized his white horse and the dark curls falling onto his collar. Then the coach clattered over the bridge and Arabella, looking back, failed to see him.

"Gracious, who could he be?" she said.

"Who could who be?" Lady Margaret asked.

"That man on horseback."

"Man on horseback? I did not see him," Lady Margaret said.

"I expect that was because he was on my side. He was very handsome. His hair was long."

"It was long?" Lady Margaret looked surprised.

"Quite long, onto his collar," Arabella amplified. "He smiled at me."

"Oh, dear, all the way up here!" Lady Margaret sighed. "You will not encourage him, please." She frowned. "In fact, I wonder if, after all, I should not take you with me to Scotland?"

Arabella glared at her. "I did not smile back," she snapped. "Besides, Papa has particularly said that he wants me to know my great-great-aunt."

"I expect he is right, since she is the only one of your mother's family who survives. It is amazing that they all died so young."

"Yes, is it not?" Arabella agreed with a little shiver.

"Child," Lady Margaret said quickly, "I did not intend to disturb you. You take after your father's family in appearance, and we are all long-lived. And, of course, there is your great-great-aunt, who is close on ninety. In fact, I think she might even be older. She was born while George the First was still on the throne, and both her niece and her great-niece dying so quickly, it's truly surprising."

"Yes," Arabella agreed a trifle dolefully, wishing that her aunt had been similarly short-lived. But she should not wish that, not even in her innermost thoughts! It was like ill-wishing someone, and she had certainly not meant to do that! Still, to be forced by that same aunt to stay in the castle with an ancient relative, rather than being with her best friend and partaking of the joys London offered, seemed indeed a cruel twist of fate. Yet that man on horseback *had* been extremely handsome, even though peculiarly dressed. And where had he gone so quickly?

Then the castle was upon them, casting its long shadow over them and, Arabella thought with a little shiver, enveloping them. Immediately that thought crossed her mind, she experienced an odd chill that could be diagnosed as fear. Yet there was no reason to fear her destination, there was only reason to regret it, which, in a sense, she still did, especially when she thought of Clemency, whose presence she missed more than she had believed possible.

Her thoughts were broken off as the coach, clattering into the vast courtyard of the castle, tilted from side to side due to the uneven stones over which it was traveling. Meg shrieked and sobbed at this unfamiliar movement and was brusquely told to hush by Rose, who had, in sharp contrast to Meg, remained calm throughout the journey. Meeting Meg's frightened gaze, Arabella suddenly realized that her abigail had been in a depressed state of mind ever since they left London. Attendant on that thought was an image of Meg talking animatedly to a young man in a servant's livery, who worked in the house next door to their own. Was he the reason for her current depression? Quite possibly. She had a moment of regret for her summary uprooting of the girl. She had never thought . . . but one did not think about the woes of servants, she decided regretfully. If Meg continued in this vein—but this thought fled as the coach drew to a stop.

In a matter of minutes, Arabella, her aunt, and their abigails were standing near a huge oaken door with a large brass knocker set higher than Arabella's head. The groom who had been assisting them out of the coach scurried over to the door and, lifting the knocker, dropped it against its plate. It fell with a startlingly loud clang. With an equally startling alacrity, the door was opened by a tall, grizzled butler, who surveyed them out of small suspicious brown eyes. He was clad in a rusty black livery, but his linen was spotless and his haughty bearing befit one who has worked in palaces. At least, Arabella thought, that was how she would have described him had she been minded to write a book. Indeed, the castle itself was more than conducive to such a volume, and certainly writing would be one way to while away the tedious hours of her exile.

These thoughts were summarily banished as the butler said suspiciously, "Ye'd be the ladies Arden?"

"I am Lady Margaret Kelley, and this is my niece, Lady Arabella Arden," her aunt said, looking surprised, Arabella thought, at his gruff mode of address. She added, "And what are we to call you?"

"I am James," he said with a smile that banished Arabella's earlier impressions. He continued, "I bid ye welcome, your leddyships. Please come in." He moved back.

"I thank you, James," Lady Margaret said graciously.

She stepped inside, hastily followed by Arabella, who had a strange and, needless to say, surprising feeling that rather than entering the castle hall, they were moving into the maw of a great monster. She hastily dismissed that analogy as singularly silly, due no doubt to her copious reading of ghost-ridden novels. Meg, she noticed, looked as timorous as she herself had briefly felt. The abigail's eyes were wide as she gazed about an immense hall with a flight of stone stairs on one side. A long table lay near the steps, and directly opposite was a huge fireplace that looked as if a whole ox could have been roasted therein.

Before Arabella could give her new surroundings another glance, the butler led them up the stairs to the first floor, which, unlike the entrance hall, was a place of dark paneled walls adorned with large landscapes beside tall double doors that, he explained, opened into the library, the music room, and the portrait gallery. At the far end of the hall lay a corridor leading into another wing, where, he informed them, Lady Knollys's suite of chambers was located.

"The mistress be old and cannot climb the stairs to the second floor where most of the bedrooms lie," the butler explained.

Gazing about her, Arabella found herself speechless with amazement and, at the same time, eager to explore this vastness. Surely the castle was larger than those to which she had previously been invited. Indeed, nothing had prepared her for it. Her father had not even given her an inkling of what she might expect. Perhaps that was not surprising, since he had first wooed her mother here and, consequently, it was associated with his all-too-brief happiness—a happiness that had ended when her mother died only hours after her birth.

Indeed, it was a marvel that he wanted to look at her, given her part in bringing his brief joy to so sad an end. Still, he had never blamed her. In fact, he had been extremely critical of friends who bitterly had held their children to account for the death of one or another beloved wife.

"After all, my dearest," he had said, "while I do miss your mother, and shall always regret her early death, I have you."

Her eyes stung with sudden tears. She wished strongly that he were with her or that he had allowed her to accompany him to France. She would miss him, and he, she knew, would miss her, but it was not the time for such regrets. The journey had ended and she was here, and must needs make the best of it . . . or rather, the most of it.

As these thoughts sped through her mind, a middle-aged woman came forward and was presented as the housekeeper. She showed Arabella and her aunt up to the second floor. Here lay their bedchambers, each with a sitting room and, wonder of wonders, a bathroom complete with water closet and running water! These amenities, the butler explained, had been laid on by Lady Knollys's late son. Arabella tried to work out his relationship to herself but gave up. It was too complicated. How, she wondered, would she keep these relationships straight? She actually envied her aunt, who, being one of her father's sisters, had not to deal with these complications.

She was still turning them over in her mind an hour later, when, with her hair combed and her gown changed, she and her aunt, similarly refreshed, followed the butler again, moving down first one corridor and then another, their goal being Lady Knollys's chambers. Once more she was aware of closed doors, high carved ceilings, and walls hung with paintings of people in quaint costumes and bearing some resemblance to each other, and to her. Obviously, she was a member of a very large and ancient clan, and she quite longed to see the portrait gallery, tantalizingly on this same floor.

Upon her comment that the immense spread of rooms appeared to be a very large space for so few people, the butler had given her a quizzical look, saying that there were some here who did not believe it to be large enough. She had not been vouchsafed any further explanations, mainly because he had been seized with a fit of coughing and by the time he had recovered, they were standing at the door to her great-great-aunt's suite of rooms.

Almost instantly after his tap on the door, that portal was opened by a young woman who stood just beyond the threshold. She was tall and very pretty in a fragile way, Arabella thought. In fact, save for a crown of red-gold hair and a touch of color in cheeks and lips, she was very pale and also extremely slender. Her gown, an un-adorned pale gray-green, was very becoming, almost matching her eyes. Fortunately, unlike most girls of her complexion, her lashes were dark and almost as long as Arabella's own, or, she ruefully admitted to herself, longer and curling at the ends, which hers did not.

As these details flashed through Arabella's mind, Lady Margaret said in some surprise, "You'll not be a relation. You're nothing like the rest of them."

Arabella frowned. As usual on occasions when her aunt was nervous or confused, she was correspondingly outspoken and brusque. Fortunately, the young woman did not appear to take her comment amiss. She said merely, "I am a relation, but extremely distant." A smile briefly brightened her eyes. "One might say that I am a mere twig on the family tree. My name is Constance Derwyn."

"We are pleased to meet you," Lady Margaret said in tones uncharacteristically indecisive. "I must ask your pardon for my confusion, but I am not familiar with this branch of my niece's family."

"I quite understand," Miss Derwyn said. "Her ladyship is anxious to see you. Will you please come in?" She pushed the door open wider and stood aside as, much to Arabella's consternation, Lady Margaret stalked rather than walked inside. Following her, Arabella had the strong impression that her aunt had formed one of her quick dislikes for Miss Derwyn. No doubt, her niece reasoned ruefully, she would find reasons for it later. Those thoughts were swiftly replaced by surprise, as she found herself in a jewel of a chamber. She had an instant impression of delicate pastel colors on walls, on striped blue and pink satin draperies, on a spread of carpet that she knew must be Aubusson, and on the silken seats of chairs, which, unless she missed her guess, came from the hand of an artisan in France. More than an artisan, she assured herself as she sent another glance around the chamber, the unknown craftsman had been an artist. She hoped that his death had occurred before the Revolution, with its destruction of so much that was beautiful about the *ancien régime*.

Before Arabella could make any further assessments, her aunt was purposefully propelling her forward to another graceful chair, a chaise longue, in fact, where propped against blue-and-peach-colored satin cushions lay an elderly lady. At first glance, she reminded Arabella of a Dresden figurine. As if, indeed, the artist had had as his model a shepherdess grown old, but still as entrancing as she had been when posed with her shepherd— many, many years ago.

Time, the enemy of all humanity, had traced lines on her pale brow and, surely, the faint flush on her cheeks was spurious. Yet her pompadour of white hair could easily have been a powdered wig rather than age's frosty touch, and her gaze remained eager, youthful, and interested. Without knowing quite why, Arabella felt the sting of tears in her eyes. Words sprang to her lips but, to her surprise, she could not utter them.

Then Lady Knollys gazed up at her out of gentian-blue eyes and said in tones as fragile as her person, "So this is little Arabella. You have your dear mother's eyes, but I would think you favor your father's side of the family."

"I have been told so, Aunt Juliana," Arabella said almost regretfully, wishing oddly that she might have inherited that fragile beauty and matchless charm. Then, like a wrap she no longer needed because the room was so warm, her regret at being forced to come to the castle dropped away, and happiness took its place. She was quite, quite sure that she would love it here.

"Yes, you definitely do," Lady Knollys said. "And that is all to the good." She sighed. "She was most fragile. I was so fond of her. As you know, your mother lived here from the time her parents died until she married your father. I had hoped to see her again, but she has never visited us."

To say that Arabella was confused by this comment was putting it far too mildly. In fact, she found herself without words, but those were supplied by Miss Derwyn, whose comforting "Not all do" proved equally confusing. Probably, Arabella decided, she was humoring her employer.

"Yes," her ladyship nodded. "That is quite, quite true, Constance dear, and there are many that I would as lief not welcome—but I was very fond of dear Anne and I should have liked to see her again."

At this moment, Arabella, glancing at her aunt, caught the latter's eye and found within its depths a confusion equal to her own. Then, suddenly, there was a knock on the door.

"Will you answer that, my dear Constance?" Lady Knollys asked. "I hope it will be Francis. I sent for him, as you know."

Hard on her request, Miss Derwyn opened the door and smiled cordially. "Ah, Sir Francis, will you not come in?"

"I thank you, Miss Derwyn. How is my grandmother this afternoon?"

"In excellent condition, Francis, dear," Lady Knollys called. "Come in and be introduced to more of your relations."

A tall young man with dark locks flowing to his shoulders entered. On seeing him, Arabella experienced a shock. Though he was now clad in garments that appeared to be made of some sort of leather, she had no trouble recognizing the laughing youth who had ridden after her coach. As she had previously noticed, he was quite strikingly handsome.

"My dear Lady Margaret and Arabella, this is my great-grandson, Sir Francis Knollys."

"I am delighted to meet you, Sir Francis," Lady Margaret said, extending her hand.

"It is my pleasure, Lady Margaret," he said courteously, as he bent to kiss her hand.

"And I, too, am delighted to meet you, Sir Francis," Arabella said, smiling up at him.

"The pleasure is mine." He bowed to her.

"You are a very fast rider, sir," Arabella could not help commenting. She received a blank look and was in turn confused. "It *was* you who passed us on the road, was it not?"

He appeared as confused as she did. "Had I been on the road," he said with a whimsical smile, "it is quite possible I would have passed your coach. But I have been in the library writing to my valet. He is currently in Paris and staying overlong. Residing with him is the portmanteau containing my garments and also his shears."

"His . . . shears?" Arabella questioned.

He touched his flowing hair. "Until he comes to clip my locks and also to provide me with a change of garments, I must continue to resemble an aborigine from the shores of my native Canada."

"I have told him," Miss Derwyn said, "that there are plenty of barbers in Richmond."

He laughed, showing strong white teeth that looked the whiter contrasted with his deeply tanned face. "And I have told Miss Derwyn and my aunt that it is as much as my life is worth to patronize a barber in Jean's absence. He is a quarter Iroquois and half a savage. He would not hesitate to scalp me were I to avail myself of services other than his own." He winked at Arabella.

"Gracious!" Lady Margaret exclaimed.

"Quite," he nodded. "It is a lamentable situation." He turned to Arabella. "Consequently, Lady Arabella, I think you must have mistaken me for someone else."

"Yes, very possibly she did," Miss Derwyn said, sighing.

Hearing that sigh, Arabella's confusion increased, and blended with it was a touch of annoyance. She did not understand the companion's attitude. Why had she corroborated his . . . She hesitated to term it an out-and-out lie, but, at the same time, unless he had a double, it must have been he whom she had seen on the road. Again, why lie about anything as minor as riding after a coach? It was very confusing, to say the least. Unless he did not want the companion to know that he had been riding after her—which opened another line of reasoning entirely. Could Miss Derwyn and Sir Francis be romantically entangled? It was certainly a possibility. Arabella found herself hoping that they were not.

These thoughts were scattered as Miss Derwyn said, "I do hope your valet will return soon, Sir Francis."

"My own hopes match yours, Miss Derwyn." He favored her with a rueful smile. "Still, in my estimation, it is time and past that the source of the confusion was removed and the—er—ghostly population of this castle sent to their eternal rest."

"G-ghostly population?" Lady Margaret repeated, staring at Sir Francis in consternation. "Surely you must be funning!"

His smile vanished. "On the contrary, I am very serious, Lady Margaret. The castle has more than its share of specters. Furthermore, as I am sure you are aware, there are those who make a profession of exorcising ghosts. I have made inquiries in the village, and I have been told of a most reputable man currently living in Richmond. I mean to see him as soon as possible."

15

Miss Derwyn tensed. "I believe you are not aware, Sir Francis, that such efforts have been made before, and to no avail."

Lady Knollys, who had been lying back against her cushions, her eyes closed, suddenly sat up and, with a rueful look, said, "My dear, new brooms sweep clean. Still, I am sure Francis will take heed of my wishes."

"Only the other day, you were telling me how difficult it is to find servants," Sir Francis gently reminded her.

"It is difficult, but not impossible. And once they are aware that the specters are harmless—"

"Harmless is as harmless does," Sir Francis commented coldly.

During this colloquy, Arabella and her aunt had exchanged another set of confused glaces. Then Lady Margaret said, "I—I have heard of haunted castles, but I had always believed such tales apocryphal."

"And so had I," Sir Francis said. "I have had, however, strong reasons to alter my opinion."

"They have been here such a long time." Miss Derwyn spoke almost pleadingly.

"All the more reason that they ought to be wafted to other spheres or wherever," Sir Francis said insistently.

"You might have difficulties or, rather, your exorcist might have difficulties in performing his duties here," Miss Derwyn said.

"I understand that he has been most successful in his dealings with the damned."

"The damned?" Lady Knollys repeated indignantly. "You'll not be suggesting that ours are damned?"

"If our so-called 'buried ancestors' do not remain peacefully grave-bound, what else can one believe?" Sir Francis asked reasonably. "Furthermore, certain of them are extremely obstreperous. I am sure you will not disagree with me when I say that they cause considerable confusion, as witness Lady Arabella's recent experience on the road."

"My . . . recent experience?" Arabella repeated. "You'll not be saying that—"

16

"That is precisely what I am saying," he interrupted. "I bear a strong resemblance to my several-times-great-uncle, also a Sir Francis, a man with an unenviable reputation."

"Still," Miss Derwyn said emphatically, "he can wreak no *physical* harm."

"Arabella, my dear, I think it is time we rested," Lady Margaret said edgily. "I am beginning to feel the effects of our journey and I am sure that you must be similarly uncomfortable." Without waiting for a response, she turned to Lady Knollys, adding, "I do hope you will excuse us. It was a long journey."

"Of course," Lady Knollys replied. "I quite understand. The terrain is quite rough in some places."

"Yes, indeed it is," Lady Margaret agreed.

"I think," Miss Derwyn said, rising, "that I had best escort you to your chambers. It is easy to become confused in this castle."

That, Arabella thought, was putting it mildly. Confusion was also reigning in this chamber and, more specifically, in her head. She said, "I do thank you, Miss Derwyn." She smiled at Lady Knollys. "It is a great pleasure to have finally met you, ma'am. I have heard so much about you from Papa."

"Ah, yes, your father . . . such a charming young man." She sighed. "They were a lovely couple. Enough, I am sure that you have given him great comfort, too."

"We are very close," Arabella agreed, nodding as, with her aunt, she moved out of the chamber. They were quickly joined by Miss Derwyn, who led them down the corridor they had earlier traversed and then into another corridor that they had not previously seen. Then, finally, they reached their chambers.

"I do thank you, Miss Derwyn," Lady Margaret said coolly and a touch condescendingly.

"It was my pleasure, your ladyship. I had best tell you, too, that the stairway that lies at the end of the hall is the one you must take to come down for dinner. No, on second thought, I think I had best send a servant to escort you thither."

"We would appreciate that, Miss Derwyn," Lady Margaret said.

"We really would," Arabella said, smiling. "This castle is very confusing."

"Indeed it is," Miss Derwyn agreed. "Even those who have lived here for centuries are, on occasion, confounded by its passageways."

"You—you cannot believe in—in the ghosts!" Lady Margaret stared at her incredulously.

"On the contrary, your ladyship, I have had ample reason to believe in them," the companion returned coolly. "Now, if you will excuse me?"

"Of . . . of course," Lady Margaret said weakly. She was silent until Miss Derwyn had walked out of sight. "I—I think they are all mad here."

"If they are," Arabella said, her mind furnishing a felicitous image of Sir Francis, "it is a most interesting madness and, after all, I am very glad that I have come. Very glad, indeed."

= 2 =

LADY MARGARET, WATCHING Miss Derwyn move down the hall, was silent until the companion had turned a corner and was lost to view. "I do not like her," she said with characteristic frankness.

Arabella tensed. Her aunt was prone to making quick judgments, and generally she was wrong. "You hardly know her well enough to dislike her, Aunt Margaret."

"She is too bold by half. She is not the lady of the manor."

"I cannot see that she has any pretensions in that direction. I am sure you mistake her."

"And I am sure that you are mistaken if you disagree with me, my dear." Lady Margaret frowned. "Very often companions get far too familiar and think themselves at home when actually they can be dismissed as easily as any other servant."

"Good gracious, Aunt Margaret, I did not notice that she was overfamiliar."

"No, my love, you were far too interested in Sir Francis—who, I fear, is far too interested in his great-grandmother's young companion."

"Oh, dear, do you think so?" Arabella asked in some distress.

"I do—and I wonder if it were not better you came to Scotland with me."

"No!" Arabella cried. "It was Papa's desire that I stay and become acquainted with my mother's relations."

"Which number two, and one of them daft; indeed, I wonder if they are not both daft. All this insane chatter about ghosts!"

"We have both known people who have family ghosts," Arabella reminded her.

"We have both known people who have *said* they have family ghosts. It is my opinion that those who prate about such matters cannot trace their ancestors back any further than their grandparents. In fact, I have heard of a man who specializes in painting 'family' portraits of Elizabethans, Cavaliers, and the like."

"Oh, dear," Arabella laughed. Then, sobering, she added, "I doubt that this particular family needs to seek its prestige through spurious ghosts."

"Lady Knollys is very, very old," Lady Margaret commented.

"She does not appear senile, and furthermore, Sir Francis also believes in the castle ghosts."

"He might," Lady Margaret said, "and again, he might be humoring Lady Knollys."

"He is certainly handsome," Arabella said.

"Yes, his barbaric costume becomes him. I wonder how it will be when he dons civilized garb and loses his lovelocks," Lady Margaret commented dryly.

"I do not believe you like him, Aunt Margaret," Arabella accused.

"I neither like nor dislike him. I do not know him; nor, my love, do you."

"I cannot imagine why you are being so critical!" Arabella frowned.

"We have seldom come among strangers, my dear."

"Since they are my relatives, they cannot be considered strangers," Arabella retorted defensively. She yawned. "I think I must rest before dinner."

"I am of the same opinion," Lady Margaret said. "It has been a double strain. First the journey and then, hard on it, our meeting with your great-great-aunt—not to mention all that daft talk about ghosts!"

"I hope there are ghosts," Arabella said. "I have never

seen any." Even as she made this statement, her mind's eye furnished an image of the man who had briefly pursued their coach. "At least," she amended, "I do not think I have."

"Since all such tales are apocryphal, I would lay you a monkey you have not." Lady Margaret smiled. "And will not!" She moved into her chamber, and Arabella hastily made use of the communicating door between their sitting rooms.

Entering her bedchamber, Arabella heard a loud scream, and found Meg standing over a pile of garments she must have just dropped. She turned a pale face toward Arabella. "I—I am ever so s-sorry, milady," she stuttered as she scooped up the fallen clothes. "You s-startled me comin' in so sudden-like."

"I am sorry, Meg," Arabella said hastily. A glance at her abigail showed her that the girl was still trembling. "Gracious, Meg, what is the matter. You are shaking like an aspen leaf."

"It—it's just that the girl wot showed me to these chambers t-told me that the castle was 'aunted by ever so many ghosts."

"If, indeed, it is haunted, Meg, ghosts cannot harm you. They can only startle or frighten you."

" 'Tisn't wot Betty wot showed me 'ere said. She told me there be buried treasure in this 'ere castle. It be guarded by evil ghosts an' anyone comin' near it meets wi' a terrible accident. She said the ghosts went an' chased one person to—to the ramparts an' made 'im leap to 'is death." Meg began to weep.

Once more, Arabella's mind's eye supplied her with an image of a smiling, animated Meg talking to the young coachman from next door. She had not displayed such animation since leaving London and Arabella had a strong feeling that the abigail's mood would last until their return. She said consolingly, "My dear Meg, we will not be here forever, you know."

"Oo's to say we—we will not, wi' all these 'orrid ghosts about." Meg's sobs melded into a wail.

"Oh, dear," murmured Arabella to herself. She hurried out of the chamber and down the hall in search of the stairs. Fortunately, her admirable sense of direction did not play her false. In a few moments, she had reached them and, running down to the first floor, she met one of the footmen and asked where she might find the housekeeper.

" 'Er chamber be at the end of this 'all, milady." He pointed to a passageway behind the stairs. "I'll show you."

"Thank you, and you'd best give me her name. I did not catch it when we came in. And you, too, must have a name."

" 'Tis Michael, milady. Housekeeper's name be Mrs. 'Unter."

Arabella had reason to be glad of Michael's guidance, since Mrs. Hunter's rooms lay near the center of a rectangular maze of passageways. She was also glad that, without being asked, the footman assured her that he would be remaining to guide her back to the stairs.

Mrs. Hunter proved, on second acquaintance, to be a small, plump woman of some forty-odd years of age. She cordially invited Arabella into a large room furnished with the same heavy carved pieces she had glimpsed upon entering the castle. There was another door, which, Arabella guessed, led into the housekeeper's bedchamber. Then, refusing the chair the woman politely offered her, Arabella quickly explained her problem with Meg and received a knowing nod.

"Aye, I had a notion your Meg weren't going to be happy here. This castle don't appeal to everyone. However, happen I know of a young woman named Jenny Field who's back from London and lookin' for a post. Mayhap ye can gi' her a try."

"I should certainly like to speak to her," Arabella said. "I imagine she has references?"

"Oh, yes, milady. I wouldn't have mentioned her if she hadn't references," the housekeeper assured her gravely.

"I am sure you would not, and I do thank you, Mrs. Hunter."

" 'Twas my pleasure, milady," the housekeeper said, smiling. "I could have her fetched this afternoon."

"Tomorrow will be time enough, Mrs. Hunter," Arabella assured her hastily. Arabella was feeling unaccountably weary and in no mood to interview a substitute abigail.

As she moved toward the door, the housekeeper came with her. "I hope Michael, or whoever brought you here, waited. 'Tis that easy to become lost in the castle." She opened the door. "Ah, Michael, lad, 'tis good you're here." She smiled at the footman.

"Couldn't let 'er leddyship go back by 'erself, Mrs. 'Unter," he said.

"Nay, you couldn't, lad."

"I do thank you," Arabella said, wondering if she had imagined a warning note in the housekeeper's voice.

"Ye'll be needin' guidance until ye know the castle better, milady," the housekeeper said. "There be all manner o' nooks and crannies to confuse ye."

There *was* a warning implicit in the woman's tones as well as her comments, Arabella decided. She would have liked to question her further on what she might really mean—but not at this moment, when tiredness, like a dark cloud, was enveloping her.

Once back in her chamber, with Michael gratefully dismissed, Arabella communicated what she was sure must be good news to Meg, only to find the girl frowning and regretful. "I 'ope she can do for ye like I done."

"I cannot hope for that, Meg," Arabella said tactfully. "There's no one who can really fill your place."

"Oooh, m-milady," Meg burst into tears. "I—I shouldn't be d-desertin' you."

"My dear Meg, it will not be for long. It will only be until Papa returns from Paris."

"Ye won't 'ire 'er 'til I can gi' 'er a look-see?" Meg spoke almost threateningly.

"Of course I shan't," Arabella said soothingly.

"An' ye won't bring 'er back wi' ye when ye return to London?"

"I would not think of it, Meg!"

"Ye might find 'er 'andier 'n me," Meg said almost accusingly.

"I could never find anyone handier than you, Meg," Arabella assured her. She added wearily, "Now, please, I must rest before dinner."

"Oh, milady, I be that sorry," Meg cried. "I wish ye were comin' back wi' me—wot wi' this place bein' 'aunted 'n' all."

Meg's procrastinations were becoming wearying. Arabella said gently, "Why do you not go down and have a cup of tea. I should like to rest for a bit."

"I'll 'elp you undress," Meg said firmly.

"Very well, Meg." Arabella swallowed a sigh.

Having arrayed Arabella in a negligee, her abigail had just left the chamber when there was a knock on the bedroom door. Stifling her irritation, Arabella hurried to open it. She found Miss Derwyn just beyond the threshold.

"I hope I have not roused you, Lady Arabella?" she said apologetically.

"No, of course not. I had not settled down for a nap yet."

"I am glad of that—though, of course, you will need your rest. It must have been a most tiresome journey."

"It was a bit tiring," Arabella agreed.

"Keeping that in mind, I will not take much more of your time. Still, there are things I must tell you—forewarned in this instance being much better than forearmed."

Arabella tensed. The companion was regarding her gravely and even, she thought, worriedly. She wondered what she would add to the warnings implicit in the speech of both the footman and the housekeeper. She said, "Will you not sit down, Miss Derwyn?" Arabella indicated a winged chair.

"I will, thank you, Lady Arabella," Miss Derwyn said taking a rather stiff chair. Arabella gratefully availed herself of the winged chair. "I understand," Miss Derwyn said, after a slight pause, "that your abigail has given notice."

"No—she has not given notice. Meg is leaving the castle, but she will return to our home in London."

"That is probably all to the good. London servants generally do not care for Yorkshire. And, of course, they early learn that there are ghosts in the castle."

"Ghosts, yes. Do you really, *truly,* believe in the castle ghosts, Miss Derwyn?"

The companion flushed. "Yes, I do—I have had . . . ample reason to believe in them, Lady Arabella. I have seen them. And to avoid the confusion you might feel upon seeing one or another of them yourself, I think I had best describe them to you. If you do not mind, of course."

"On the contrary, Miss Derwyn," Arabella said rather dryly, "I should be interested to hear about them."

"I can tell by your tone of voice that you are inclined to doubt me—and, in the interests of preserving your mental equilibrium, I feel it best that you listen carefully to what I have to tell you."

"I have already admitted my interest, Miss Derwyn," Arabella said rather edgily. "I pray you will continue."

"Very well, Lady Arabella. The ghosts of the castle number five."

"F-five!" Arabella exclaimed, staring incredulously.

"Five, Lady Arabella," Miss Derwyn nodded. "There are three men and two women, or, if you prefer, five specters. The oldest of the five are actually the youngest—mainly because they were slain fighting for Richard the First in the Holy Land. They are brothers, and their names are Fulk and Roger. They died, I understand, within minutes of each other. Being eighteen and nineteen at the time, they did not take kindly to death and they haunt the castle corridors jousting with broadswords.

"They generally arrive on the stroke of midnight and remain until the first sign of dawn. They harm no one. Then there is Lady Blanche, born in 1399 and brought to the castle after the Battle of Agincourt. She, I am given to understand, was happily wed to a young nobleman in her native France. He was slain by Sir Bertram Knollys, who took Lady Blanche as a spoil of war. He forcibly married her and she bore him four children—three daughters and a son. Shortly after the birth of that son, she stabbed Sir Bertram while he was sleeping. Subsequently, she strangled her three daughters and tried to slay her baby son. A nurse prevented that and Lady Blanche killed herself by leaping from a tower window."

"My goodness!" Arabella breathed. "And she haunts the castle?"

"Yes, and is doubly damned since she appears to wish to communicate with one or another member of the family—but speaks only an antique French, understood by none, not even her fellow ghosts."

"That is a pity," Arabella commented.

"Few would agree with you, Lady Arabella. I might mention that, on occasion, Lady Blanche can be very dangerous. She is, I might add, very fair, very beautiful, and is clad in a long white gown."

"Aren't they all?" Arabella asked facetiously. "Specters, I mean."

"No." Miss Derwyn frowned. "The gown is of her period—with wide sleeves and heavily embroidered in gold. The material is called samite."

"And how can she be dangerous in her disembodied state?" Arabella inquired.

"I speak only from hearsay."

"Are members of the family the only ones who meet with these specters?" Arabella asked.

"No, some few people have seen them—but not often. The ghosts seem to be able to make themselves visible at will. And certain of them are more available than their fellows."

"You have mentioned three. Who might the other two be?"

"There is Lady Helena, who lived during the reign of Charles the Second. She was slain by her irate husband for infidelity with his younger brother, who was, as it happens, also Sir Francis Knollys, or perhaps I should call him Francis, the first." Miss Derwyn flushed as she added, "They bear an astonishing resemblance to each other."

"Oh? And how did Sir Francis die?" Arabella asked, feeling that she knew the answer before it was vouchsafed.

Miss Derwyn corroborated that feeling as she said, "He was killed by his brother. A servant saw the—er—guilty pair together in the stable loft and led his master to the spot."

"And was he amply rewarded?" Arabella asked with a slight shudder.

"No," Miss Derwyn replied, with a satisfaction Arabella did not quite understand. "He was dispatched by the same sword that slew Sir Francis and Lady Helena."

"And does he, too, haunt the castle?" Arabella asked interestedly.

"No, certainly not," Miss Derwyn said disdainfully. "He was not a member of the family."

"Poor man," Arabella commented. "No doubt he'd anticipated a large reward."

"He received his reward," Miss Derwyn said coldly. Then, for some reason, she flushed. "I have told you about these ghosts because you might see one or another of them. They have been viewed by other family members and, on occasion, by strangers, too, depending on their own peculiar awareness or, apparently, the desire of the ghosts."

"I see—and the current Sir Francis wishes to send them to their eternal rest?"

Miss Derwyn frowned. "Yes, and he is not the first member of his family to try to get rid of them. However, all such attempts have failed. And those who have initiated them have come to regret their—interference."

A slight shiver coursed down Arabella's back. "They have retaliated?"

"Would you not retaliate if someone chose to drive you from your home?" Miss Derwyn demanded with an unexpected passion.

Several questions coursed through Arabella's mind—one in particular being predicated on the companion's peculiar attitude, which, to her mind, seemed as if she were actually defending these shades. However, she said merely, "I expect I would. How have they—er retaliated?"

"One young man fell to his death from a turret. That happened a hundred years ago. Some sixty-five years ago, a young woman went mad and spent the rest of her days locked in a barred chamber. She lived until the age of eighty-four and never regained her sanity."

"Gracious," Arabella breathed. "It would be best, I expect, to assure them one meant them no ill will."

"I think such reassurances would be greatly appreciated," Miss Derwyn said.

"Have you mentioned these matters to Sir Francis?" Arabella asked.

"I have," she said sharply.

"And he does not believe you?"

"He believes me, yes, and is determined to make a clean sweep of them—as he said. I am sure you heard him."

"Oh, yes, of course. I was so caught up in your account that I forgot. He mentioned a professional exorcist. Has such a person ever been employed here?"

"Yes. Over a hundred years ago, when the family was still of the Papist persuasion, a pair of priests were summoned to perform an exorcism. However, nothing came of it."

"They would have used bell, book, and candle?" Arabella asked.

"Yes, that is right." Miss Derwyn looked at Arabella with some surprise. "They did employ that method—to no avail. In fact, I understand that both priests were reduced to abject terror and died within the month."

"Gracious! Has the current Sir Francis been informed about this unfortunate occurrence?"

"Of course. Unfortunately, it has failed to deter him," Miss Derwyn said rather sharply. "He will need to live and learn."

"Or he might not live—and in consequence, learn nothing." Arabella suddenly shuddered.

"Let us hope that it will not come to such a pass. He is the last of his line and were he to die—"

"Oh, dear," Arabella said, sighing.

"Quite," murmured the companion. "But enough, I do wish to warn you not to wander about late at night. As a member of this family, there is no telling what you might see."

"I do thank you, Miss Derwyn. I think I must convey that information to my aunt, as well."

"Pray do," Miss Derwyn said. "Of course, she might not see anything, not being a Knollys."

Into Arabella's mind suddenly flashed an image of the young man who had briefly pursued their coach—the young man in black, with peculiarly cut garments, who had borne such a striking resemblance to Sir Francis. Was it possible that she had glimpsed the first Sir Francis? She said tentatively, "I expect that the—er—deceased members of the family do not appear in broad daylight?"

"They prefer the hours after sunset, Lady Arabella. But they appear when they choose to appear. That is why I have felt it incumbent upon myself to warn you. And, in common with their kind, they are not always well-disposed toward the living."

"You have already suggested that they might not be, and . . ." She paused for Miss Derwyn had suddenly started to cough.

Miss Derwyn quickly pulled a handkerchief from the bosom of her gown and put it to her mouth, taking it away as the paroxysm ended and replacing it in her bosom—but not before Arabella had glimpsed a spot of blood on it.

"I—I beg your pardon," Miss Derwyn said when she could finally speak. "This castle is conductive to colds."

"I am sure it must be," Arabella agreed. "Fortunately, I rarely suffer from them, myself."

"That is fortunate," Miss Derwyn said. "I think," she

added, "that I have interfered with your rest long enough. I had best return to Lady Knollys. And, please, I beg you will wait until a servant comes to show you and your aunt down to the dining room."

"We shall, of course," Arabella assured her, thinking privately that there was something peculiarly sinister in the companion's warning. Yet, at the same time, it was also peculiarly intriguing, to the point that she could no longer decry the loss of Paris or, indeed, the joys of London!

= 3 =

"Gracious! An escort to the lower floor?" Lady Margaret commented. "Well, I expect we would have trouble finding the withdrawing room. Without having seen very much of this castle, I think it might be rather like Chinese boxes."

"Chinese boxes?" Arabella questioned confusedly.

"One inside of the next, generally of different colors and certainly of different sizes—though my analogy might be considered misleading."

"I see," Arabella said, thinking that her response was not quite a lie, but only a ruse to avoid one of the lengthy explanations that Lady Margaret was unfortunately far too fond of providing. Undoubtedly, the castle did have its complications and, she thought with a sudden surge of pleasure, hard on her aunt's departure she would have ample time to explore it. Unlike Lady Margaret, Arabella possessed an adventurous spirit and, also unlike her aunt, she did not require constant companionship.

Once Lady Margaret left the castle, Arabella was quite sure her unfortunate abigail would be bombarded with observations—the thought of which made her even happier that she had reached a destination more felicitous than she had ever anticipated. She flushed slightly as—hard on that thought—the image of Sir Francis flickered in her mind's eye.

With that gentleman in mind, Arabella decided to wear a gown fashioned by a well-known mantua-maker, whose prices were commensurate with her fame. Still, there was no doubt that she was an artist, Arabella thought once Meg had fastened the minute buttons at her wrist into their tiny loops. A shimmering green silk, the gown was a close match to her eyes. And its round neck was very flattering. She had elected to wear her pearl necklace and matching earrings—simple but effective, her mirror assured her.

Fortunately, her curls needed only a few strokes of the brush, rather than the annoyance of curlpapers, something about which dearest Clemency constantly complained. Her mirror showed her color in her cheeks—a faint flush that she hoped her aunt would not mistake for rouge! She frowned, remembering the near-crisis engendered by Lady Margaret on the evening of her initial visit to Almack's.

On coming to her chamber, her aunt had marked the flush of excitement on her cheeks and had angrily accused her of using rouge! Despite Arabella's vociferous denials, Lady Margaret had insisted that Meg wash Arabella's face and, subsequently, she had examined the cloth! Arabella's father, waiting downstairs, had come up to discover the reason for the delay and had been very angry with his sister. As for herself, Arabella had solemnly vowed never to speak to her aunt again—as long as she lived! That resolution, however, had been broken within minutes of making it.

A tap on the door banished these unpleasant memories as Meg, opening that portal, disclosed Lady Margaret looking her imposing best in gray silk and amethysts. "Are you ready?" she asked.

"As you see," Arabella said, and immediately regretted that response. Undoubtedly, Lady Margaret would believe her rude.

Fortunately, her aunt did not appear to notice. "Let us go down to dinner, then," she said, adding with a slight shudder, "I do not like this castle."

"You have seen very little of it, Aunt Margaret," Arabella said in some surprise.

"I have seen quite enough. It is, to my mind, uncommonly gloomy."

"I would think that most castles are rather gloomy," Arabella commented.

"On the contrary, the castle to which I am bound is delightfully bright and airy. I do wish you were coming with me. You have met your great-great-aunt, which was the main reason for this detour. And I doubt that you will see much more of her, given her great age and indifferent state of health."

The handwriting on the wall was limned in colors no one could mistake, Arabella thought. She decided she must be very firm if she were to hold out against persuasions that sounded far more like commands.

"Papa was extremely insistent that I come to know my mother's family. It is something I can hardly accomplish in a night and a day, Aunt Margaret."

"To my thinking, you will not be seeing much more of your great-great-aunt. She is far too old and too frail to tolerate much company."

"Then why did she invite me here?" Arabella asked reasonably.

"I am not sure that she did. The invitation might have been of your father's arranging."

"If that were so, he would certainly want me to remain," Arabella said.

"You would enjoy Scotland, my dear."

"I am sure I will prefer it here. I am weary of traveling and—" Before she should produce more fuel for that argument, there was a tap on the door.

Meg opened it. A young man in the neat, dark garments of a servant stood outside. He was carrying a candle. "If you please, your leddyships," he said politely, "I am here to escort you to the drawing room."

"Oh," Lady Margaret said. "Very good. We are ready." Turning to Arabella, she added unnecessarily, "Come, my dear."

The stairs to the lower floor were, as Arabella recalled, broad. Midway down, they ended in a small landing and subsequently angled into another, shorter, flight. On reaching a hall still bathed in the glow of the northern sun, glimpsed through two tall arched windows, Arabella was momentarily surprised at the strength of that celestial orb. Then, as their guide led them into another corridor, she remembered that the sun would not set until nine o'clock or even later. A stronger spill of light from three more windows showed them paneled walls that, Lady Margaret commented, must have been superimposed over the stone of an earlier century.

Gazing at the windows, Arabella found that they looked onto lawns bounded by a barrier of tall pines. Since she had not seen them before, she guessed that they were at the side or back of the castle, and decided that once her aunt left, she would make an effort to get her bearings. One could easily become lost in the plethora of passages that, she imagined, were to be found throughout this vast structure, home to generations of people—many with conflicting ideas for its improvement.

Before she could dwell any longer on the intricacies of castle-building, their guide turned another corner, bringing them to tall double-doors. Opening one, he stood aside to let them enter.

They found themselves in a most striking room. Though it was not lofty, it managed to convey a feeling of spaciousness and dignity. This was due partly to its very considerable length and partly to the numerous stone-mullioned windows, which allowed views of a terrace and quaint old knot garden and, beyond them, the massive outline of the Pennines, rising in stark grandeur against the setting sun.

Deeply interested, Arabella looked about her. The room must have been built by an Elizabethan Knollys, she decided. It had an elaborately carved plaster ceiling and the typically intricate carved paneling of the period. There were even two fireplaces, she noticed with amusement, to warm each end of the room

Only one was alight this evening, and Aunt Margaret gave a small exclamation of approval and walked over to stand in front of the cheerful blaze.

Arabella followed her, noting the many small touches of exquisite taste in the various furnishings. Undoubtedly the work of her great-great-aunt, she decided, remembering the elegance she had seen in Lady Knollys's boudoir. In the midst of these observations she heard the door open again and, on turning toward that portal, she was pleased to see Sir Francis.

He quickly bade a good evening to her aunt and, on turning toward her, gave Arabella a most appreciative smile.

"Good evening, Sir Francis," she said.

"And a very good evening to you, Lady Arabella," he said warmly. "I hope that I am not too bold in saying that you and your aunt add a finishing touch to this lovely room."

Though she wished he had not felt it necessary to include her aunt in this encomium, Arabella said softly, "I would never consider such kind words bold, Sir Francis."

"Nor I." Lady Margaret smiled.

"I am pleased to hear that. Coming from so savage a shore, I often find myself at a loss in polite society," Sir Francis remarked.

"And I, Sir Francis, have a strong suspicion that your comment borders on prevarication," Arabella dared to respond.

"Arabella!" Lady Margaret stared at her in shock. "Really—"

Before she could conclude her protest, Sir Francis flung back his head and laughed delightedly. "You are singularly discerning, Lady Arabella."

"I thought I might be," Arabella observed with some satisfaction.

"Arabella!" Lady Margaret gave her a reproving look. "You see," she said, turning to Sir Francis, "my little niece is all unspoiled."

Arabella's teeth clicked together, barring the use of her tongue in a comment she longed to utter, had not wisdom proved the better part of valor. Instead, she said with a deceptive mildness, "Will Aunt Juliana and Miss Derwyn be joining us, Sir Francis?"

He nodded. "Yes, Miss Derwyn told me that my great-grandmother will make one of her rare appearances."

"Oh, lovely," Arabella said excitedly. "I found her so very facinating."

"Yes, she is, rather," Lady Margaret agreed.

"And she is still so very beautiful," Arabella breathed.

"Indeed, she is. A porcelain lady, delicately fashioned," Sir Francis commented.

"Oh, that does describe her! Also she looks like a portrait of a Georgian beauty," Arabella said.

He smiled. "As it happens, there is such a portrait in the library, opposite that of her late husband. He must have been almost as beautiful as my great-grandmother."

It was on the tip of Arabella's tongue to say that men were not beautiful—but on looking at Sir Francis's felicitous features, she decided not to voice a comment that was certainly erroneous and that he might take as a personal insult. "I must visit the library," she contented herself with remarking.

"Yes, you certainly must," he agreed. "There is also a notable collection of books to be found on its shelves. Though they are mainly from the last century, there are a substantial number that have survived from the sixteenth and seventeenth centuries, and there are a few that date back even earlier. They are in surprisingly good condition, too."

"Oh, that is lovely. I truly enjoy reading," Arabella exclaimed.

"The volumes from the eighteenth century should prove of particular interest to you, Arabella," Lady Margaret commented dryly, "since it was then that the gothic novels you are fond of reading first made their appearance."

Meeting Sir Francis's rather amused gaze, Arabella felt her cheeks burn. Happily, she was prevented from a comment that must have caused sad repercussions once they were alone, for, in that same moment, the door was opened and Lady Knollys, leaning on Miss Derwyn's arm, entered the chamber, to be followed almost immediately by James, the butler, who bowed to his mistress, saying "Dinner is served, milady."

After a quick exchange of greetings, Sir Francis escorted the ladies to a vast chamber in which stood a long table covered with a fine linen cloth. On either side were set four chairs, their high carved backs padded with dark-blue velvet. At either end were armchairs of the same design. To Arabella's eyes they looked curiously thronelike. Another glance took in a heavily carved and extremely long sideboard to the left, and to the right three arched windows filled with stained glass. Each showed a shield of blue on which was emblazoned a gold dragon with a wrinkled snout and a long red tongue curling between sharply pointed fangs. Obviously, it was, Arabella thought with a little shiver, the emblem of her mother's house.

An upward glance showed her a high ceiling with a fine crystal chandelier. Despite the daylight outside, and the lighted candles in the chandelier, there was only enough light to see the each other's faces, not enough to dispel the gloom that darkened the far reaches of the chamber.

Miss Derwyn led Lady Knollys to the head of the table and pulled back the chair.

"Oh, no, no, no, my dear," she protested softly. "I always feel as if I am sitting on a throne. Let me have one of the side chairs. They are ever so much more comfortable. In fact, I will take the one next to the—er—throne and let Francis occupy it instead, since he is the man of the family."

Arabella, who had been looking directly at her great-great-aunt, caught the gleam of a coquetry as charming as it was unexpected. For some reason she could not explain, she was amazed and touched by the beauty that settled over Lady Knollys's features as if, indeed, a friendly fairy had waved the wand that restored her youth. For some reason she did not quite fathom, she darted a look at Sir Francis and found his eyes suspiciously bright, as if he, too, had noticed and had been struck by sensations similar to her own.

Before she could dwell longer on these feelings, Miss Derwyn had approached the chair beside that of Lady Knollys, and Sir Francis had hurried to seat her. As Arabella wondered which chair she should choose, she found her great-great-aunt's eyes upon her.

"Please," Lady Knollys said, smiling at her, "you will sit across from me, Arabella. And Lady Margaret, will you take the chair next to that of your niece, please?" She visited a gracious smile on Lady Margaret.

As Sir Francis pulled out Lady Margaret's chair and subsequently her own, a side glance at her aunt told Arabella that she was not pleased by an arrangement that left her facing Miss Derwyn. In medieval terms, she was, at least in her own estimation, seated below the salt. Arabella bit down a laugh. It was utterly ridiculous for her aunt to be concerned over protocol at such a time. Indeed, she had never known her to be quite so toplofty. Then, darting a commiserating glace at Miss Derwyn, which was also a silent apology for her aunt's untoward rudeness, Arabella was utterly amazed by the girl's beauty.

Miss Derwyn had also elected to wear green—a shimmering silk, simply cut, but a perfect match for her large and very beautiful green eyes. Indeed, Arabella, possessing eyes of a similar hue, somehow felt that her own had sadly shrunk, and though she did have long lashes, the companion's eyelids were thickly fringed with even longer lashes, curling at the ends and as dark as her own. Unfortunately, Arabella's lashes were sadly straight and, furthermore, in common with herself, Miss Derwyn's face was an exquisite oval, and had the added attraction of high cheekbones, something Arabella did not possess. Constance Derwyn's mouth was full and red, and her auburn hair seemed to be of many colors, from light amber to deeply dark. Worn in coronet braids, it reminded Arabella of the crown it was designed to emulate. Much as Arabella hated to admit it, Miss Derwyn was quite incredibly beautiful and, she thought unhappily, no one was more aware of that than Sir Francis!

He had also known her for two unobstructed weeks! Arabella felt her cheeks grow warm as the possibilities attendant upon that realization became depressingly clear. An additional warmth invaded her as she realized that she was beginning to regard the companion as a rival! That, of course, was utterly ridiculous! She hardly knew Sir Francis and, attractive as he certainly was, who knew whom he might have left behind in his native Canada? Arabella judged him to be in his mid-twenties and, if he was anything like the gallants who thronged London, he would not have restricted himself to merely male companionship. Did they have opera dancers in Canada? Her mind did not supply any ready answers. Furthermore, it was quite possible that he was already affianced.

These melancholy thoughts were happily dispersed by the arrival of servants bearing massive silver trays on which were dishes under silver covers. The food proved succulent enough to suggest that a most accomplished cook held sway in the kitchens. In fact, the meal was so very tasty that conversation did not really commence again until after the sweet—a rich and singularly delicious confection—had been served and delightedly devoured.

"Your cook is a marvel, Lady Knollys," Lady Margaret commented.

"Yes, we are very fortunate in having her services," Lady Knollys replied. "Actually, she started as a kitchen maid training under Robert, our late chef. Upon his demise, she took his place. He taught her all he knew."

"Certainly, she has proved an apt pupil," Lady Margaret said.

"More than merely being his pupil, she has improved upon his work," Lady Knollys said. "Though, on occasion, I miss Robert. He was here for so many years, you see."

"My father knew him," Sir Francis said. "I heard tales of his cooking in Canada, and truly it made my mouth water."

"Your father," Lady Knollys sighed. "A dear, dear boy . . . You have much the look of him." Another sigh escaped her. "I do hope you have not inherited his temper, but I am rather sure you have not."

"I do have a temper, sad to say," Sir Francis said, smiling a little ruefully. "But I can safely say that it ignites far less often than that of my late father."

To say that Arabella was intrigued by these comments was putting it far too mildly. She was burning with curiosity. Only her good breeding restrained her from voicing the questions piling up on her tongue. Again, she was glad of her decision to remain in the castle. Once she knew Sir Francis better, enlightenment must needs follow. She smiled at him, but, sad to say, he was gazing at Miss Derwyn, who, in turn, was smiling at him.

"My dear Constance," Lady Knollys protested softly, looking at Constance's untouched plate. "Do eat your dessert. As usual, you have barely touched your dinner."

"I have had quite enough, Lady Knollys," Miss Derwyn assured her with a smile.

"If you are to retain—" She paused as the table shook slightly while overhead the crystal drops of the chandelier clashed together.

"Gracious." Lady Margaret paled. "W-what was t-that?"

Arabella found herself swallowing air bubbles in fright. Not only had the table shaken, she had felt movement beneath her chair. A glance at Sir Francis showed her that he, too, appeared startled by this untoward shaking. However, Lady Knollys, she noticed, appeared quite composed.

"It is nothing," she assured them calmly.

"N-n-nothing?" Lady Margaret echoed. "It was an earthquake! I—I felt the floor m-move under my f-feet."

"Yes, on occasion it does, and has for many years." A soothing note had entered Lady Knollys's voice. "When I came here as a bride, I, too, was quite startled by these occasional movements and my dear husband had some difficulty soothing me, I remember." She laughed. "I had a feeling that we must be catapulted off the hillside, and he told me that would never happen. I am proof, I believe, of that. In fact—" She paused as a crystalline clatter of chandelier drops attested once more to that peculiar movement.

"Is—is it some manner of—of earthquake?" Arabella questioned nervously.

"No, my dear, my husband told me it was just settling. These hills are honeycombed with mine workings. The Romans, you know, mined lead in these parts."

"I would think, Grandmama, that after so many years, it would be *settled*," Sir Francis commented.

"Yes, my dear, I quite agree," Lady Knollys said, smiling at him. "But, as I have said, the castle does remain intact, and so have I. But, my dear Constance, I think I must retire."

"Yes, of course, we'll go at once, Lady Knollys." Constance rose quickly, and in another moment had gently assisted the old lady to her feet.

"I will bid you good evening, my dears," Lady Knollys said softly. "It has been such a lovely day, and it has also been such a pleasure to welcome you, Arabella, and you, Lady Margaret, to my home."

"It—it has been our pleasure, too," Lady Margaret said rather tremulously.

"Yes, it has," Arabella agreed, glad that she sounded considerably calmer than her aunt.

A chorus of warm good-nights and wishes for her peaceful slumber were expressed by her three guests, but once Lady Knollys and her companion had quitted the chamber, there was a veritable babble of comments from Lady Margaret and Arabella, the one decrying the quivering of the castle and the other defensively downplaying it—the while Sir Francis was obviously biding his time until the ladies ran out of breath.

Finally, the flood of comment ceased and he was able to say easily, "I would not be alarmed. My grandmother has lived here for close on seventy years, and I am sure that you also know that generations of the Knollys family have occupied the castle. The family chronicles are in the library and some of our historians have prated of a possible cataclysm, and have subsequently gone to their graves without experiencing such a catastrophe. And so, I am sure, will we."

"I—I intend to—to leave on the m-morrow," Lady Margaret said in quavering tones. "And—and you, Arabella, will go with me!"

"No," Arabella said. "You heard what great-great-aunt Juliana told you—she has survived a good many years without witnessing such a catastrophe as you fear, and my mother grew up in this castle!"

"My father was born here," Sir Francis said calmly. "I would think that we are in no danger. One of my mother's family visited the coast of upper California where, he told me, there are frequent earthquakes, and they happen not once in a generation but many times a year! Still, many Spaniards have come to settle there. As I said, my grandmother has lived in this castle for sixty-seven years, and while age may have taken its toll—earthquakes have not."

"That is certainly obvious—since the castle does remain intact," Arabella said. Meeting his eyes, she read admiration in them.

"And I am of the opinion that it is dangerous and, had your father been aware that the castle shakes, he would never have permitted you to come," Lady Margaret retorted.

"I am sure he must have known," Arabella insisted. "I want to stay. I want to get to know my mother's family, and Papa wanted me to know them, also. That is why he sent me here!"

"That was not precisely why . . ." For some reason Lady Margaret flushed, adding hastily, "But I pray you, let us not argue about it now. It is late and I am weary, as you must be after so much traveling.

Arabella was not in the least weary, and she quite longed to remain and converse with Sir Francis. However, at this particular moment, it were better to be conciliatory, she decided.

"I expect I am a little tired," she conceded, deciding to plead encroaching sleep once they were upstairs. Her aunt, Arabella strongly suspected, was determined to renew their argument concerning their hasty departure—as soon as the sun rose. And, indeed, to refute those arguments, Arabella needed a clear head and a strong determination to follow her father's wishes—no matter what arguments her aunt initiated! Consequently, sleep in this instance could only be her ally. With a smiling backward glance at Sir Francis, she followed Lady Margaret from the chamber.

= 4 =

MEG, APPEARING much less lugubrious than she had earlier in the day, helped Arabella out of her gown and arrayed her for the night. Busy brushing Arabella's hair, she said, "The girl wot'll be waiting on you 'll be here tomorrow shortly after noon, Housekeeper says. But," she continued almost angrily, "if you and her don't suit, I'll stay."

This ingenuous speech alerted Arabella to the fact that her abigail was of two minds about resigning her position, however briefly. She said gently, "I will put up with her during my stay at the castle, but I am sure she will not have your expertise, Meg."

"Mayhap I ought to stay," Meg murmured.

"No," Arabella said hastily, confronted with the thought of the abigail's megrims during the several weeks they might be remaining at the castle. "I think it is better you leave. I will certainly not be remaining here indefinitely. I cannot like the idea of a haunted castle, myself."

"N-no." Meg shuddered. "No more can I." She shuddered a second time, her expression revealing that her fears had come rushing back as Arabella had hoped they would; Meg's fancies would hardly add to a stay Arabella was beginning to contemplate with considerable pleasure.

Shortly after her abigail had arrayed her for the night, Arabella, coming to her windows, looked out on a dimming sky incongruously bejeweled with points of light that, as the darkness increased, would reveal the fact that they were stars. Then, the half-disk caught among the dark branches of the trees would look more like the moon. Even with daylight lingering so long, she found the view much to her taste.

" 'Ah, what light through yonder window breaks'— n'er did I believe in that encomium until you appeared at your window, my lady fair."

Startled by the soft, insinuating male voice, Arabella looked down and met the dark gaze of Sir Francis. But surely she must be mistaken. He could not—not on such a brief acquaintance—be staring ardently up at her. Yet, judging from the intense expression in his moon-illumined eyes, it certainly appeared as if he were! Also, it was far, far too early in their acquaintance for him to address her in these flowery terms!

She said repressively, "I think you must be joking, sir."

He said quite seriously, "Upon mine honor, I am not. 'Tis regrettably seldom that I am treated to such incredible beauty."

Arabella stiffened and took a step backward. "I think you wax far too extravagant, sir," she said chidingly.

"How may I convince you, fairest of the fair, that I have spoken naught but the absolute truth?"

Obviously, he had a warped sense of humor and was teasing her, she decided crossly. "It is time you should seek your own chamber and your bed, Sir Francis," she snapped.

His eyes widened, and he smiled broadly. "And suppose if, most radiant of beauties, I should prefer your chamber and your bed?"

She stiffened. "Obviously, you are inebriated, Sir Francis." Moving back, she closed her windows and stood against them, feeling both angry and disappointed. Earlier in the evening he had drunk very sparingly. But, obviously, he had subsequently imbibed a great deal more wine or, perhaps, brandy. And by himself, too, she suspected. Unless, she thought reluctantly, he had later repaired to Miss Derwyn's chamber.

Scarcely had this most unwelcome suspicion entered her mind than she was startled by a sudden chill that descended upon her like an all-enveloping cloak. At the same time, a soft voice remarked, "By Satan, I could not have believed you any more beautiful than you appeared, framed in your window, but I was mistaken. You are much, much more beautiful. Indeed, in the words of the Bard of Avon, I must needs call you 'most radiant, exquisite and unmatchable beauty. . . .' Viola was speaking partially in jest to that simpering female, Olivia, but I, not being disguised, give you only the truth."

Arabella, gazing up into dark, laughing eyes, was both frightened and confused. "How did you arrive here so— quickly?" she faltered. "It—it is not possible."

"N'er ask the how or why of it, my beautiful. Suffice to say that I am here—a wanderer from 'night's Plutonian shore,' come to bask in the sunlight of your incredible loveliness."

His voice was soft and, though he stood perilously close to her, she had no real sensation of that proximity. As this confusing realization swept through her mind, he sighed and, with a wistfulness she found entirely surprising, he said, "Alas, my dearest, we should have met much, much earlier, or much, much later."

"I am of the opinion that we ought not to have met at all, Sir Francis," she said coldly. "Were my aunt to come in, I should have considerable difficulty explaining your presence. Indeed, I—I do not quite understand how . . ." She paused. The moon had come out from behind a cloud and the man before her seemed to waver in its brightness, a brightness that appeared not only to envelop him, but to shine through him. With a little cry of fright, she stepped back. "You—you are—"

"Francis Knollys, my little love," he murmured. And, bowing, he vanished.

"Ohhhh," Arabella screamed, and felt the room whirl about her. She knew herself to be in danger of swooning! She had an odd feeling that her ghostly visitor might have deliberately engendered that sensation. Bereft of the powers he had possessed in life, he needed to impress the females he might still covet, in ways that must render him unforgettable, even to the unobtainable. After drawing several breaths, she finally managed to regain her equilibrium.

A moment later, her door flew open again, and there he was, standing on her threshold. He was dressed differently. He wore shirt and trousers only. His feet were bare. Backing away from him, she cried, "Go—go back to whatever hell you came from!"

He did not move. Regarding her confusedly, he said sharply, "What manner of nonsense is this, pray?"

At that irate question, Arabella's fear fled, to be replaced by shaky laughter—laughter bordering on the hysterical. "It—it was not you—it was he—" she gasped, and with a strong effort managed to quell her laughter.

"Ah," the anger faded from his face and, moving farther into the chamber, he put his arm around her—a solid arm, firm on her shoulders. "You have . . . encountered one of our 'buried ancestors'?"

His arm was proving most sustaining, enabling her to achieve a laugh with no hint of her previous hysteria. "I—I cannot believe that he is buried very deep."

He, too, laughed. "You are uncommonly brave, Lady Arabella."

"Brave?" she repeated. "When it was my screams brought you here?"

"You are not screaming now and, given your experience with our peripatetic ancestor, I cannot think that there are many females who would calm down so quickly." Then, before she could respond, he added, "Your aunt sent a message, informing me that you will be accompanying her to Scotland on the morrow—which, I imagine, must afford you a certain sense of relief."

Despite her recent fright, Arabella found herself truly angry at her aunt's overweening determination to bend her to her will. She said sharply, "That was never the plan, Sir Francis. I will be remaining here as my father wanted."

He regarded her quizzically. "Despite your encounter with our ghostly ancestor?"

"I am not afraid of him," she assured him.

"Ah, I am pleased to hear it. May I hope, then, that you will come riding with me tomorrow? I feel that we ought to know each other better—so that your confusion will be happily laid to rest."

She wished he had issued the invitation without a qualifying reason. Still, she quickly assured herself, she was being far too impatient. After all, she had known him no more than a few hours. She said, "I would love to go riding with you, Sir Francis."

"Very good. Shall we say midmorning? After last night's excitement, I wish to look in on my grandmother. Perhaps you will come to see her too?"

"I shall. I am already very fond of her. She is quite wonderful, I think."

"I agree. And—" Before he could continue, there was a knock on the door.

Arabella moved to open it and, on pulling it back, she found Miss Derwyn on the threshold. She was wearing a long wine-colored velvet robe and she was looking concerned. "You screamed, I am told, Lady Arabella?" she remarked without preamble. Then, looking beyond Arabella, her eyes widened. "Sir Francis!" she exclaimed.

Arabella felt her face burn, but before she could proffer an explanation for her cry, as well as for the untoward presence of Sir Francis, he had said coolly, "She screamed, Constance, because she had had quite a fright. I heard her and that is why I am present."

"Yes, that is quite true," Arabella corroborated. She added, "Will you not come in?"

"Thank you, I shall," the companion replied coolly, stepping over the threshold. "And might I know the reason for this fright, Lady Arabella?"

"The noble Sir Francis, the first, decided to pay her one of his so-called courtesy visits, Miss Derwyn," Sir Francis explained in chill tones. "The need for an exorcist is, I believe, increasing."

Miss Derwyn visibly tensed. "I cannot agree," she said hotly. "He—*all* of them are quite harmless."

"I disagree with you. In any case, there is no reason why those who come to the castle should be intimidated, if not harmed, by these unhallowed creatures!"

"There is not a harmful bone in Sir Francis's body!" Miss Derwyn retorted angrily.

"I would imagine that there is not a whole bone in his body. But still he manages to menace the living, and the sooner he is dispatched to his—er—eternal rest, the better it will be for those who must needs dwell in the castle. Not everyone, Miss Derwyn, shares your tolerance for the restless dead."

"You will find that Lady Knollys is in agreement with me," she cried.

"Ah, but I am of the opinion that it can be changed, despite what I suspect are your best efforts to the contrary."

"It was none of my doing, Sir Francis," the companion retorted. Turning, she left the room, closing the door quietly behind her.

"Gracious," Arabella exclaimed. "She does seem to be uncommonly tolerant of ghosts."

"Does she not?" he said grimly.

"I expect she is used to them—living here," Arabella commented. Then she tensed. "It was not you followed our coach today." With a nervous little laugh, she added, "It was Sir Francis, the first."

"I fear you are right, but had I been riding in that same vicinity, I think I must have followed that coach myself."

Meeting his dark gaze, Arabella felt a heavy pounding in her throat. But, before she could frame an answer, he had added quickly, "I fear I am in no condition to have invaded a lady's chamber." He cast a rueful glance at his garments. "If you will please excuse me . . ."

"Of course, and I do thank you," Arabella murmured.

"It was my pleasure," he said, swiftly letting himself out and closing the door softly behind him.

Arabella remained where she was, her mind in a turmoil! So much had happened, so very quickly. She hardly knew what to think; no, that was not entirely true. She had reached at least one strong conclusion—one concerning the nonghostly Sir Francis. Of all the gentlemen she had met, he was the most attractive. And, furthermore, she had a strong feeling that he was as attracted to her as she to him.

On that felicitous thought, she suddenly found herself extremely weary. It was time to retire for the night and, she hoped, dream of Sir Francis II. Still, her excitement at the evening's events was such that she was sure she would not be able to sleep. Contrary to these expectations, Arabella fell asleep immediately her head touched the pillow.

There was someone shaking her and sobbing in abject terror. At first, Arabella thought she must be dreaming, but the shaking continued and the sobbing grew louder. Opening dazed eyes, she blinked at a quivering candle flame perilously close to her face. Shrinking away from it, she met Meg's frightened stare.

"Wha'sit," she mumbled.

" 'T-'tis them, milady," Meg sobbed. "T-they be on the—the stairs."

"They?" Arabella blinked herself awake. Then, as awareness returned to her, she exclaimed, "What are you doing here in the middle of the night?"

"Oh, milady, I wakened an' wanted to see wot time it was an' came down to look at that big clock wot's at the top of the stairs an' there they was."

"They?" repeated Arabella.

"F-fightin' they be . . . an' none to . . . to s-stop 'em."

"They? Who are they?" Arabella asked again.

"I doesn't know, milady—but they be powerful angry. Oh, milady, they got to be stopped. 'Appen they might k-kill each other 'n' everyone in this 'ere c-c-castle."

Rising as hastily as she might, Arabella followed her shuddering abigail into the hall. "I do not see . . ." she whispered.

"They be over there." Meg moved to the stairwell and,

following her, Arabella looked down and saw a pair of husky young men in knee-length tunics. Each was ferociously wielding an immense, bloodstained broadsword. Up and down the lower stairs they went and then, to her horror, a sword pierced the body of one combatant and was pulled back as the wounded man, in turn, thrust his sword into his enemy. Much to her amazement, both young men appeared to be in high good humor, and in another moment, they had dashed down the stairs and disappeared from view. It was then that Arabella realized there had been no clash of steel on steel, and though both had appeared to cry out, their mouths opening and closing and their features working, neither had made a sound!

"I—I t-think t-t-they b-be ghosts," Meg wailed.

"Shhh, Meg. I am quite sure they are," Arabella agreed. "And we should be grateful they are. Think of the noise they would be making if they were not!"

"T-they be d-demons from 'ell?" Meg moaned.

"Hush, child, go to bed, now. They have no power to harm you," Arabella said more confidently than she felt.

"But 'oo be they?" Meg began to cry again.

"I'll explain in the morning," Arabella promised wearily. She saw her abigail to the door that led to the servants' wing and waited until the girl had timorously climbed the stairs leading to her room. On coming back into her own chamber and falling wearily back into her bed, she did not think she would sleep. Not with the images of that ghostly pair churning before her mind's eye. Contrary to her expectation, oblivion again came as soon as Arabella's head touched her pillow.

She dreamed of riding over a long stretch of grassy sward. Oddly, she was not wearing her new, stylish habit of green Merino cloth, fashioned for her by Mrs. Bell, whose husband owned and edited *La Belle Assemble*. Instead, she was clad in a gown made from a material that appeared to be silk—heavier silk than any she had ever seen before. It was also long and voluminous and she was wearing a high, peaked headdress.

She was angry—more than merely angry—agonized

and furious as she cried out strongly at the man who rode beside her—a tall man in armor, smiling at her. She did not like his smile. It was lascivious and boded further ill for her. She had seen it—just before he first possessed her, taking her against her will! And now she belonged to him, and he was taking her to a destination she had never seen before; just as she had never seen this country that was not her own, and which she had hated even before seeing it. She longed for her own home, and the young man she had seen struck down by a sword wielded by this great boor of a soldier. He had found her by her husband's bed, had heard her agonized sobs as she viewed the cruel end of one she had loved all her life. And he had laughed, and unmindful of her struggles, had placed her before him on his saddlebow.

"I will be revenged," she murmured.

Arabella had known, even in her dream, that the words she uttered were in a language not her own. She opened her eyes. The mind images vanished as she stared out the window and, much to her dismay, found rain beating against the glass, and in her ears, the mournful howling of the wind.

Obviously, it was not a morning for riding, and for a moment she was not sorry about that. She had been riding all the day and most of the night through a strange country, where people spoke an uncouth language and where jeers, and what appeared to be epithets, were shouted at her from a scurvy-looking crowd on the muddy roads over which her horse was bearing her.

Subsequently, Arabella was amazed at the images that had traveled through her consciousness—remnants of a dream that had, from the looks of her sheets and blankets, kept her restless all the night.

A tap on her door startled her. "Yes?" she called edgily.

"Ah, good, you are awake." Lady Margaret came in. She was dressed for traveling and, visiting a disapproving look on her niece, she said brusquely, "You are still abed, I see. You'd best dress, and quickly. We leave for Scotland shortly."

"Scotland!" Arabella echoed. "No—" she cried, adding foolishly, given the circumstances, "I am not expected in Scotland."

Her aunt frowned. "You are not *expected* in Scotland, true, but I still want you to come with me. I do not like this place. It could fall—crumble, whatever. I'll not have an easy moment if I leave you here."

"It was Papa's wish that I be left here," Arabella said firmly. "You know that."

"He will understand my scruples. I cannot imagine he would want you to remain here—not after last night."

"You heard Lady Knollys say that the castle shakes. Yet she remains alive and appears in remarkably good health considering her age—and she has lived here well over sixty years!"

"All the same—" Lady Margaret began.

"No!" Arabella exclaimed. "I cannot think what Papa would say were he to know I had deliberately ignored his instructions, which were, if you remember, to remain here."

"He does not know about the castle. I cannot think why your poor mother did not tell him!"

"Of course he knows. He courted my mother here. I will not go, Aunt Margaret." Arabella glanced at the windows. "It is not raining hard now, but it could get worse. The weather is changeable. Shouldn't you be on your way?"

"I want you to come with me," Lady Margaret said insistently.

"And I am bound to obey Papa's instructions," Arabella countered, obstinately.

Quite suddenly, Lady Margaret capitulated. "Very well," she sighed, "I cannot remain here arguing the morning away. As you have pointed out, the rain could increase." She shook her head. "I can only hope that your stubbornness will not bear poisoned fruit."

Lady Margaret's peculiar analogy sent a little shiver through Arabella, one she reluctantly diagnosed as fear. She was suddenly aware of a strange wish to leave with her aunt, but she would not give in to it, not with the image of Sir Francis Knollys large in her mind's eye. She said, "I have your direction in Scotland. If any of these prognostications come true, I will write to you."

"Have you thought, my dear, that you might not be in any condition to write?" Lady Margaret frowned.

Another shiver went through Arabella, but coupled with it was anger. "Since Lady Knollys has lived here since her arrival as a young bride, I feel that two months will not see me caught in the rubble of a fallen castle, nor drowned in its moat!"

It was Lady Margaret's turn to shiver. "I hope you are right, Arabella." She glanced out of the window and frowned. "I do believe that the rain is increasing. The roads in Yorkshire leave much to be desired and—Enough, I must go."

"I do wish you a safe journey, Aunt Margaret," Arabella said.

Coming to the bed, Lady Margaret bent over and kissed her niece on the cheek. "Fare you well, my dear," she said, sighing. "You have my direction. I pray you will write."

"I promise I shall, Aunt Margaret. And may I hope that I will soon hear from you?"

"You shall, of course." For a moment, Lady Margaret looked as if she wanted to instigate yet another argument, but then, with a sigh and a shrug of her shoulders, she hurried out of the chamber.

Arabella was conscious of relief blended with an odd sense of foreboding, a feeling she hastily dismissed as being based on Lady Margaret's ravenlike croakings. The fact that her aunt was leaving cheered her immensely. For the first time in her life, she was happily minus a mentor and could do as she chose. She found her sense of foreboding fading from view, much as the carriage bearing her aunt to Scotland would soon be doing. Not even the rain, which precluded a ride with Sir Francis, could obliterate the relief she was currently experiencing. At long last, she was her own person and, within reason, she could do as she chose!

=== 5 ===

AN HOUR AFTER her aunt's departure—when she was sure Lady Margaret would not return—Arabella rang for Meg. Belatedly, she remembered the girl's decision to leave, and remembered also that the housekeeper had recommended a replacement. Consequently, she would have to interview the new girl. In that circumstance, it was just as well it was raining. No, it was not! She had really wanted to ride with Sir Francis, who was her main reason for refusing to leave the castle. And—

Meg's arrival ended Arabella's cogitation. She said abruptly, "That girl be here."

"To whom might you be referring, Meg?" Arabella asked in some confusion.

"The girl wot'll be replacin' me." Meg's jealousy showed vividly in her expression as well as her tone.

"We have already agreed that she is merely a temporary replacement," Arabella reminded Meg gently. "Have you met her, then?"

"Aye, that I have. She wanted to come wi' me now, but I told her she'd have to wait 'til I was finished dressin' you."

"Do you like her, Meg?" Arabella inquired.

The girl hesitated before saying grudgingly, "She be well enough. From around these parts she be, but was workin' in London. I wonder wot made her leave. P'raps she were dismissed."

Arabella swallowed a burgeoning smile. Her maid was obviously torn between a strong desire to leave and a strong fear that her replacement might be preferred to herself, despite the years she had been in Arabella's service. She said gently, "I hope that was not the case, but I am sure that no one could serve me better than you."

Meg's face clouded. "I could stay," she said.

"No, I think it is best that you leave. I know you are not happy here. You will feel much more yourself at home in London, I am sure."

"I will that, milady," Meg said, brightening slightly. "But I wish you was comin' wi' me, 'stead o' stayin' wi' them wot were on the stairs."

"Heavens, I had almost forgotten about them."

Meg looked patently disbelieving. "I don't see how anybody could forget something like that. Could see right through 'em when the moon hit 'em, 'sides they was evil—goin' at each other the way they was."

"Come, even if they are evil, they are past wreaking their spite on the living. In a sense, my dear Meg, they are only shadows."

"I don't like 'em," the girl insisted. "I wish you'd've gone wi' Lady Margaret."

"I happen to like the castle, Meg," Arabella said. Once more, the handsome features of Sir Francis flickered in her mind's eye. She cast a regretful glance at the rain-streaked window. It seemed to her that the rain was even heavier than it had been earlier. Actually, her aunt ought to have remained until it lessened, but Lady Margaret obviously preferred muddied roads to shaking castles. Perhaps it was a pity that Meg could not have gone with her—certainly, they were of the same mind. Meg, of course, would have to remain until the new girl was interviewed, but even if she did not quite suffice, Arabella was determined to allow Meg to return to London.

Three-quarters of an hour later, Jenny Field, brought to Arabella's chamber by a glowering Meg, stood in front of Arabella, gazing at her hopefully. She was a small, slender girl of, Arabella guessed, nineteen or twenty. She was also very pretty and her expression was bright—but she did not seem above herself and, fortunately, her references were excellent.

Questioned about her previous positions, she mentioned two—one, where she had stayed four years until her mistress remarried and went to live in Gibraltar with her naval husband, and another, where she had remained a scant three months due to illness at home. She had arrived in Yorkshire only a month since, to nurse her sick mother. However, her mother's health had improved and she could now leave her and find work.

"There be a lady who wants me, but not until autumn," she explained. "So I would be ever so glad if I could work here."

"And I would be pleased to have you come—though I must explain that I will be returning to London in a matter of two or three months."

The girl's face lighted. "Oh, that'd suit me just fine," she breathed. "I do thank you, milady."

"It is I who should thank you. I am sure we will do very well together, Jenny. You may go now. May I hope that you will return this afternoon?"

"Oh, I will that, milady. At what hour shall I be here?"

"Three o'clock would suffice."

"I'll be 'ere—here," Jenny said.

Having summoned Meg to see Jenny out, Arabella looked after her with a smile. Obviously, the abigail was trying to improve her speech, suggesting that she wanted to better her position in life. Arabella could not fault her for that. Indeed, she hoped she would be successful.

"I don't like her," said Meg on her return. "Has a bit to much to say for herself. P'raps I ought to stay wi' you."

"No," Arabella said quickly. "I really cannot agree with you. She seems willing enough. Of course, she cannot possibly replace you, but certainly she will do until I return home."

"I hopes you don't regret it, milady," Meg said in tones that gave the lie to those hopes. "I wonder wot she'll do when she sees the ghosts?"

"I hope she will take them in her stride," Arabella said

out of great relief. Hiring a servant was often a lengthy process. Many girls who applied were not at all satisfactory, something one could tell immediately. However, she had warmed to this girl at once, and the fact that she had remained in one position for four years was proof of Jenny's ability, she thought. Furthermore, she did not have the strong Yorkshire accent that was so difficult to understand. She spoke quite as clearly as Meg; in fact, her speech was much more grammatical. Indeed, she was really a find!

Clad in a becoming white muslin gown, Arabella wrapped a new paisley shawl about her shoulders in deference to the castle chill and, on being directed to the housekeeper's room, she made arrangements for Meg's departure that afternoon.

Actually, she found herself more distressed over the pending absence of Meg than that of her aunt—though she could comfort herself with the fact that Meg, even more than her aunt, had displayed a strong dislike of the castle—a dislike that, in common with Lady Margaret's, was based on fear. Arabella did not understand their fears. There was little those ghosts could do, bereft of their bodies, as it were. Her memory of Sir Francis, caught in the light, had been most instructive. No matter how solid he had appeared, he was only a shadow without substance, as was that ferocious young pair of swordsmen of the previous evening.

"Three . . ." she murmured.

She had seen three out of the five resident ghosts—and what were the remaining pair like? She would not dwell upon them at this time. She would go and pay her respects to her great-great-aunt, and then— She loosed a sigh at the thought of that missed ride and then shrugged. There would be other better days, and then they would ride. She was quite sure Sir Francis would issue a second invitation.

Meanwhile, she would pay her respects to Lady Knollys. It was possible that Sir Francis would be with her. She found the chamber with an ease that surprised her. She had tapped on only one other door before discovering the right one. However, once Miss Derwyn had opened it in answer to her knock, she put a finger to her lips, whispering that Lady Knollys was still asleep.

"I should have told you that she seldom rises before early afternoon—one or two o'clock generally," she explained.

"I do hope I have not disturbed her," Arabella whispered.

"Oh, no, you have not. And I am sure she would like to see you later this afternoon—say, three or four."

"Very well, I will return then," Arabella said, smiling.

On leaving the chamber, she felt very much at loose ends. Then she remembered that Lady Knollys's rooms lay on the first floor, and on the other side of that same floor were the library, the portrait gallery, and the drawing room. She wished she had asked Miss Derwyn where to find them. Fortunately, she recalled traversing a corridor at the end of the hall. She hurried back in that same direction. On going down another hall, toward the stairs, she passed a double door and noted that one part of it was slightly ajar. She was about to push it open all the way, but paused, wondering if it was another bedchamber. Then she remembered being told that only Lady Knollys resided on this floor.

Putting out a tentative hand, she clutched a doorknob set almost as high as her head. Then, for some reason she could not quite explain, shivers of nervousness traveled up and down her back and she wondered if she should venture inside.

He who hesitates is lost. The saying coursed through her brain. Impulsively, she pushed the door open and only just kept herself from clapping her hands for joy, while laughing at her incipient fears. She had found the portrait gallery! Joyfully, she stepped inside, gazing with wonder at the numbers of portraits lining the long stretch of wall facing her.

They were many shapes and sizes—from small oval miniatures to huge equestrian canvases and family groups. There were also several full-length portraits. Another look showed her that there was a certain resemblance between many of the subjects. She resolved to start at the far end on her left—where an all-embracing glance showed her that there were two marble masks and beyond these a crude portrait that she guessed to be of great antiquity.

Moving away from the door and going in the direction of the marble masks, she came to a startled stop. They looked faintly familiar, and in another moment she realized she had seen them before. Where? Examining them closely, she realized that they resembled the faces of that ghostly pair she'd seen silently jousting on the stairs.

Coming closer to the masks, she found a yellowed card on which was written in flowing Spencerian script, their names and dates, as well as the name of the battle in which they had perished—the Siege of Acre, Jerusalem, 1191—fighting under the banner of Richard I, the Lionhearted. Their ages at the time were eighteen and nineteen.

Tears for those aborted young lives filled Arabella's eyes, and then she smiled. No longer could she decry those ferocious combats on the stairs. Obviously, the mock battles echoed the pleasure they had known so briefly—in life.

Moving farther along the gallery, she studied more Knollys portraits—a thin young man who lived briefly in the reign of Henry IV, and another whose dates showed him to be a subject of Richard II. She found herself more interested in the Tudor portraits with their narrow suspicious eyes and bulging bodies—it appeared that some members of her family had emulated the eighth Henry. Then, a little farther along, she met the smiling eyes of Sir Francis. He looked much as he had looked the night before, save that he wore a long curled wig. However, his clothes were different. He wore a jacket with elbow-length sleeves over a shirt that fastened tight at the wrists. There were several rings on his fingers. Glancing at the dates below the painting, she read: "1642–1677."

"Thirty-five," she whispered, and realized she was staring at the likeness of the first Sir Francis, not the second. Somehow, she was not surprised at his early demise.

"But I was mightily surprised—though I should have known my brother was a damned stick, else he'd n'er believed in the so-called honor of his bride, wed after she'd spent two months at court!"

"Fie, Francis, fie, to make mock o' me—when I felt the steel that dispatched you also, and my lifeblood upon my new gown!"

" 'Twas the gown, my sweetest Helena, not my shed blood in the stable loft, that infuriated you. You'd hoped to pull in a better catch at court and to strangle the Villiers, if you could. But our sweet Barbara proved too big a fish for you to land—and so you shared the stable loft with me, who was naught but your poor brother-in-law."

Arabella, her ears filled with disembodied voices, felt shivers coursing up and down her spine. Her heart was pounding heavily as she looked about her, seeing nothing save in her mind's eye, which furnished her strange images—the one of a frowning Sir Francis and the other of a young woman whose curling brown hair had straws stuck in it. The woman's low-cut gown was much disarranged and, horror upon horror, blood seeped from a wound in one plump, half-exposed breast and stained the bosom of a gown fashioned from violet silk.

"Ah, I had hoped to find you here."

Turning swiftly, Arabella looked up into Sir Francis's smiling face. A scream threatened to escape her, but in that same moment, she saw his buckskins and could say with a great burst of relief, "You! I thought for a moment you were the first Sir Francis!"

He nodded. "Your ability to see them must prove confusing, and I, for one, find it far too confusing. The dead have no right to intrude upon the living."

"I expect it is some manner of penance that they serve," Arabella said.

"Let them serve it in other regions," he said shortly.

"They seem harmless enough," Arabella commented mildly.

"Had they been harmless, they would not be here, filling our minds with their silent chatter."

"Silent . . . chatter?" she mused. "Yes, it does drift through the mind like thoughts."

"Precisely." He frowned.

"I heard two of them just now—a woman and a man. Sir Francis, again."

"Shall we say, rather, Francis, the first?"

She laughed. "I think we must."

He said soberly, "He is best avoided."

"I should much prefer to avoid him, but—"

"I understand." He frowned. "As he was in life—so he is in death."

"I expect it was her husband killed him," she said, and in that same moment she saw the full-length portrait of a very pretty young woman. She was clad in a gown of yellow silk, cut low over her full breasts. Her brown hair was arranged in the artfully disarranged curls that were the fashion of the Restoration. "There she is!" Arabella exclaimed excitedly. "Only, she was wearing violet silk, and there was blood on it."

"You are right. I have been going through the family papers. Her husband did kill her; he found them—"

"In the stable loft," she said, nodding.

"True—a groom, hoping for advancement, so the papers say, alerted him. He was subsequently slain for his tale-bearing and, I expect, his knowledge of her infidelity."

"Alas, the bearer of bad news. But how dreadful, his own brother, too. A tragedy, indeed."

"More travesty than tragedy," he said wryly. "And we, both of us, must be grateful that the babe she earlier bore her husband had much the look of his father. By some odd trick of heredity, I am heir to my several-times-great-uncle's features—though not his proclivities."

"There's none here I resemble," Arabella said, and then frowned. "Yet I had a strange dream last night."

"Could you describe it?"

"I think so. It was very vivid—I seemed to be riding a white horse, and beside me was . . . a tall man in armor, whom I did not like. Oddly, I wore a satin gown and some kind of tall hat with a veil attached. I was very angry and, at the same time, utterly miserable. I was going somewhere—I did not want to go—and someone I loved was . . ." She shivered. "He was dead and . . ." She paused, staring at him confusedly. "I do not remember anything more. No, there is something more I remember—from the dream. I vowed to avenge him—the poor dead man."

He gazed at her intently. "She bore her captor four children, three girls and a boy. The last was but a babe in swaddling clothes," Sir Francis said. "She killed her three older children and her husband as well, stabbing them while they slept. She would have slain the baby but was prevented by his nurse, who struck her down. Subsequently, she was walled up alive in the castle—no one knows where."

"Who was she?" Arabella asked.

"Lady Blanche de Courcelles, a spoil of war brought home from Agincourt by Sir Bertram Knollys, who had found her tending her wounded husband and had slain him in front of her."

"Poor woman," Arabella said.

"I'd not waste any pity on her," Sir Francis said brusquely. "She had the character, if not the scope, of a Messalina." Then, as if to change the subject, he said, "Has anyone told you of the lost treasure?"

"Treasure!" Arabella exclaimed. "The buried treasure that is supposed to be hidden here. Was it she who brought it?"

"Yes."

"What sort of treasure was it—or do you not know?"

"Yes, I know," he said, sighing. "Generations of our family have searched for it in vain. By all accounts, it was a rich trove of gold and jewels. It is said to be hidden within these walls. If you share some memories with Lady Blanche, perhaps you'll learn if she was the one who hid it, and where. But I doubt it. She'd not be so kind to her captor's descendants."

"His and her own," Arabella said.

"Most unwillingly her own, or so say the chronicles of the time. It was none of her doing that her son survived."

"No," Arabella agreed, feeling . . . but she was not sure of her feelings as she continued, "had he been in the chamber with the others, she'd have cut his throat first of all. She was primed for it. She wanted his death more than any of the others, for he was the heir!" She shuddered. "Why? Why do I have such knowledge of that twisted mind?"

"You share a heritage with her."

"I wish I did not." Arabella shuddered.

"I would imagine it is time-diluted to a drop. But enough! Do you see what I see?"

"W-where?" Arabella asked nervously, casting a wary look about her.

Sir Francis laughed. "You must pardon me for startling you. I am not speaking of our tiresome ancestors. Rather, I meant the sunlight on the floor. It is coming from the window over there." He gestured broadly. "Would you care to go riding now? The path may still be damp, but it has not been raining overlong. Perhaps you would like to see some of the grounds?"

"Oh, yes, Sir Francis," Arabella breathed. "I should truly love to go riding, and yes, again, I am most eager to see the grounds!"

"Good." He smiled.

"I shall change immediately. Where can we meet?"

"I shall wait for you in the lower hall—near the front door."

"Thank you. I promise you, I shall not be long." She hurried out of the portrait gallery.

Some twenty minutes later, attired in a dashing blue habit, Arabella hurried down the stairs to the front door, hoping that Sir Francis would be there as he had promised, yet full of inexplicable fears that he might not have waited for her. It was unlike her to be so on edge. She could not remember a time when any young gentleman had kept her waiting. In fact, it was quite the other way around, as she had at times intentionally dallied over

64

dressing, even to the point of changing one gown for another so that her escort, cooling his heels in the drawing room, and possibly grinding his teeth, would be all the more pleased at her belated arrival.

With not a single exception, the gentlemen who had pursued her had swallowed their impatience and greeted her with a combination of relief and joy. Her father had often chided her for what he called her "deliberate provocations." No doubt he would be extremely surprised were he to know her state of mind at this moment—but Sir Francis, notwithstanding his peculiar dress, was quite, quite different!

She was exceedingly glad they were cousins—even more glad that the relationship was not so very close. Though it often happened in her circles, she was of the opinion that first cousins should not marry. Then she flushed, amazed that thoughts of marriage with Sir Francis had so quickly crossed her mind. She hardly knew him and yet she was looking forward to a happy future spent with him! That was ridiculous! She knew nothing about his previous connections. Quite possibly, in Canada, another female held these same thoughts, and with far more than a very brief acquaintance on which to base them.

He was waiting for her in the hall. His eyes widened at the sight of her, a hopeful sign, she thought happily.

"I do hope I have not kept you waiting too long, Sir Francis," she said, thinking privately that perhaps she ought to have kept him waiting longer.

He said, "You were uncommonly quick, my dear."

She noted that he had changed out of his buckskins into a dark jacket and commented, "I see you do have another coat with you."

He shrugged. "It belonged to my grandfather; apparently James produced it. He feels it is more respectable for me to go abroad in this than in my buckskins."

They shared a smile, and Arabella said, "I am so eager to view the grounds."

"And I am eager to show them to you," he said. "It is

truly surprising that you have never visited the castle before."

"I expect that Papa did not want to come—mainly because the castle holds sad memories of my mother. She died bearing me—she was no more than nineteen."

He shook his head. "That is sad, indeed. You must have had a lonely childhood."

"No, there was my aunt and my father. Also, I was sent to school in Bath. I had lots of friends there. I am sorry my mother died, but one cannot miss what one has never known."

"That is true enough," he said thoughtfully. "It is worse to possess a father with a roving eye and unbridled temper, and a mother whose stock of grievances . . . But enough, the past has passed."

"Oh, dear," Arabella said regretfully. "I am sorry. I fear you are speaking of yourself. I wish you might have been happier."

"I have been happy enough in my time. Canada might appear to be a strange and savage place to those nurtured in England, but it is beautiful! One day . . ." He suddenly flushed, adding hastily, "Come, I have had the horses brought round." Moving to the door, he opened it and Arabella, preceding him, saw two horses held by a smiling groom.

She came to a startled stop as she noted that one of the animals was most peculiarly marked. There were great brown splotches on his white body, or was it great white splotches on his brown body? She was not quite sure. His mane, she noticed, was also a mixture of brown and white. The other horse was chestnut in hue and appeared quite spirited. Or was it merely registering surprise?

"Ah, I see Jacques is willing and more than ready to go," Sir Francis commented as the brown and white horse moved restlessly and struck the ground with its hoof.

"Jacques—is that your horse's name?"

"It is. He, by the way, is a pinto, and he is named after

Jacques Cartier, who discovered the St. Lawrence River in Canada. A most beautiful body of water—at least to my thinking."

"Have you seen the Thames?" Arabella asked.

He shook his head and smiled at her. "It is a sight I have as yet been denied. I disembarked at Liverpool."

"It's a pity you did not see the river—and London, too."

"I agree, and I am loath to admit that it was vanity kept me from so doing." He smiled, his teeth very white against his sunbrowned face. She had not noticed that he was so dark, and she was oddly pleased—for his coloring heightened the difference between himself and his several-times-removed uncle. His features were truly beguiling, and beside him the late Sir Francis was a very pale shade, indeed. However, he had made a comment she did not quite understand. "Vanity, sir?"

"I did not wish to be thought a nine days' wonder, and my valet had left me immediately we docked. There was a great crowd, and we were separated. At length, after searching for me in vain, he and my luggage took coach to London, and thence to Dover and subsequently Dieppe."

"Dieppe?" she repeated.

"He had been bound for France to see relations for a brief stay. It was from Dieppe that I had his abject apologies, badly spelled, but on the whole coherent. So, I remain as you see—without my wardrobe, but with my horse, which, of course, he did not take."

"That is particularly fortunate for your horse, Sir Francis, since I understand that horse meat is considered a great delicacy in France. I doubt they could have resisted your unique steed."

"Lord, I knew that and had forgotten it until you reminded me. I hope you've not dined on steed steak, Lady Arabella."

"I have never been to France and, in consequence, have missed that particular delicacy, Sir Francis," she said, smiling up at him.

"You are strictly a lady of London?"

"Oh, Papa, my aunt, and I have traveled to Brighton several times. Papa is interested in architecture, and there is the Pavilion. I do not know if you have heard mention of it, but—"

"I have—even in our distant provinces. We receive newspapers from London—so we have read about the Pavilion. Do you admire it?"

"Well, no, not really, though people rave about it. But Papa says I am right and that it is an architectural nightmare." She flushed, thinking that this was scarcely a comment the daughter of a diplomat should be making. "I mean . . ."

"I imagine you meant exactly what you said—or rather what your father said. Such rumors have spread across the seas. Also, we have heard that the Prince Regent's taste borders on the flamboyant. And . . ." He paused as his horse snorted and tossed its head. "Ah, Jacques is becoming impatient—and I am sure that Grievance," he pointed to the other horse, "is similarly eager to be off."

"G-Grievance, sir?" Arabella questioned in some surprise.

"Aye." He smiled. "I have called her Grievance because, unless she is off and running, she is a most restless lady. She is currently demonstrating her displeasure because we have not yet mounted."

Arabella laughed. "We must sweeten her disposition, then."

"Yes, we certainly must," he agreed.

"Oh!" she exclaimed as he suddenly, and with remarkable ease, lifted her into her saddle. "You are very strong, Sir Francis."

"You are very light, Lady Arabella!" he commented, settling himself into his saddle. As they rode companionably side by side, Arabella said, shyly, "Do you know, Sir Francis, since we *are* cousins, I do think you could call me plain Arabella."

He shook his head. "No, that is quite out of the question."

"Is it? Why?" she asked, wondering nervously if she had been too bold.

"Because," his gaze rested on her face, "I could never call you *plain,* Arabella."

"Oh!" She flushed and laughed, liking that elliptical compliment. "You are very kind to say so, sir."

"I am not in the least kind. I am merely being truthful. And you must call me Francis, Cousin Arabella."

"I shall—F-Francis," she agreed shyly.

"Ah, that is much more comfortable, Arabella."

"I agree," she said warmly.

"Now, I must tell you that the road through this part of the grounds becomes very narrow and overgrown. I think it better that rather than trying to ride side by side, you follow me for the moment."

"I do agree that it does seem to be getting rather narrow for two," she told him truthfully, if unhappily.

Still, even if they could not converse for the moment, it was pleasant to be in his company. She smiled, wondering what her father would think. She had strong suspicions regarding his decision to send her north. Since being presented at court in June, she had spent very little time at home. In fact, now that she thought about it, her days and nights had been full and, more than once, he had remarked that he feared for her health—nonsense, of course! She had been in the very pink of condition, able to dance the night away, and would have risen the following morning for their rides—if it had been allowed.

Arabella pulled a face. Much to her chagrin, her aunt, acting under her father's orders, had forced her to leave routs, dances, and dinners early. Even the rides in the park, when she had been with one or another young man and, of course, her aunt, had been, she felt, unreasonably curtailed.

Fortunately, this ultimatum failed to discourage her swains. Numerous bouquets were constantly sent to her and, furthermore, there had been near-quarrels among the gentlemen who called on her. One young man had actually challenged another to a duel—in her presence. Her father, who had witnessed this altercation, had hurriedly intervened, sending them both packing with some well-chosen and extremely biting comments on their manners and morals. Subsequently, he had actually *blamed* her for leading them on—which was, as she had earnestly assured him, ridiculous since she had cared for neither!

"The sooner you are bespoken, the better," he had grumbled. "Is there no one you can like above half?"

Had Sir Francis been in London, she would have been able to give her father an affirmative answer. The moment that thought crossed her mind she tensed, telling herself that she was being utterly ridiculous! They had met *yesterday,* and already she was building airy castles for two!

They had rounded another bend in the road. Looking ahead, Arabella tensed. Sir Francis was no longer directly in front of her. Where had he gone, and more specifically, where was she, she wondered confusedly? Hard on the heels of these thoughts, came annoyance. While she had been deep in thought, he had ridden farther ahead, and without the courtesy of informing her where he was going—or was she being unfair? Obviously, he had believed her directly behind him and she, daydreaming, had not really been paying attention to him or to where they were going. The road was curving and probably he was just around the bend. She urged her horse forward and then tensed.

To her left she could see a little medieval chapel, now in a slightly ruinous state. All around were tombstones of various styles and dates. She glanced at the inscription on the nearest one and realized that this must be the Knollyses' family chapel, where most of her mother's family lay buried. She recalled her father speaking of it. In that moment, and with a neigh that sounded like a shriek, her horse reared and, throwing her to the ground, sped away!

=== 6 ===

Shocked and confused, Arabella lay where she had fallen, staring up at the sky. "Sir Francis—" she called, and then chided herself for her foolishness. He had been nowhere in sight. Where could he have gone? Had he believed she was following him? Yet, surely, he must have glanced over his shoulder once or twice.

At the beginning, he *had* looked over his shoulder and subsequently she, lost in thought, had not kept her eyes on him. Yet it was very odd of him to have so summarily deserted her, she decided, anger taking the place of confusion. She sat up and, gazing about her, she paled. She had fallen perilously close to one of the most massive tombstones—a miniature copy of a Greek temple—and, had she been any nearer, there might easily have been a tombstone erected for her!

Staring about her, she could see nothing but the moss-bedecked tombstones on all sides of her, and she began to feel rather frightened. At that moment, she heard the sound of hooves and was extremely relieved. Sir Francis was here after all. Perhaps . . . Her speculations fled and fear took their place as she saw the riderless pinto dashing through the trees to her left!

Her lurking anger vanished. Sir Francis, too, had been hurt, and where could he be? Had he, indeed, less fortunate than she, been thrown against a tombstone?

At that moment, he came toward her, his dark eyes filled with concern. "You have fallen. 'Tis unfortunate."

"Yes." She stared at him dazedly, but essayed a smile. "I rarely experience such mishaps as having a horse throw me—and yours, too, must have done the same. I saw the pinto dash past."

She got to her feet, gazing at him a trifle indignantly. He ought to have helped her rise. However, she reasoned quickly, he, too, had fallen and was probably in no condition to aid her. "Were you much hurt, Sir Francis?" she asked.

He shook his head. "There's little can hurt me these days," he assured her. "But with you, 'tis a different matter. Were *you* hurt?"

"No, only a bit shaken. I wonder what frightened the horses?"

"Surely you must know that most horses are timorous creatures. They hear what mortal ears cannot."

It was an odd way of putting it, she thought. "You are implying," she said, half facetiously now, "that the shades of our forebears wander through this graveyard? I thought they were all restricted to the castle."

"No. They may go where they choose and when they choose. Such freedom do they yet possess."

"And you, Sir Francis, are of the opinion that they possess far too much freedom?"

"On the contrary, fair maid," he said soberly. "I am of the opinion that they do not possess enough."

"Oh?" she questioned in some surprise. "You have changed your mind, then?"

"No—hold! You must take care," he said quickly, as she stumbled and nearly fell.

"I can see that I must," she replied coldly, wondering why, if he hadn't been injured, he had made no attempt to come to her assistance. In that moment, she realized they had reached the edge of the graveyard. She turned to speak to Sir Francis and, much to her surprise, she found that he had gone!

Indignation warred with confusion and consternation. Obviously, his upbringing in that savage land from which he hailed had not stressed the amenities. Still, earlier on, he had been quite courteous. Perhaps his fall had been more painful than he had admitted. And where, exactly, was she now? Looking ahead, she loosed a sigh of relief as she saw the great bulk of the castle in the near distance.

On reaching the front door of that mighty edifice, she slammed the knocker against its plate with a strength rising out of her anger and hurt that Sir Francis had so summarily left her. Fall or no fall, he should have been able to guide her to the house.

Remembering her initial impression of him, she grew even more indignant. She had been drawn to him—exceedingly drawn to him, in fact. But obviously he was more than half a savage and— Her thoughts came to an abrupt conclusion as the butler opened the door, gaping at her with a mixture of surprise and relief.

"Oh, milady, we were that worried about ye, wi' your horse comin' back by itself. Were you much hurt?"

"I'll not die of it," she snapped, and then quickly added, "I do thank you for your concern. I had a fall, but it was not overly painful."

"I am pleased, milady. There be rough spots on the grounds hereabouts."

"So I have learned," she said, sighing. "And . . ." She paused as Miss Derwyn came into the hall, stopping short as she saw Arabella.

"Oh, you are back, then," she said in some relief. Then her eyes widened. "You have mud on your habit and a tear on your sleeve."

"Have I?" Arabella glanced down at herself. "I did not notice. It must have happened when I fell."

"You fell?"

"Got tossed from her horse, she did, Miss Derwyn," the butler explained, and then stiffened at a knock on the door. As he hurried to open it, Miss Derwyn walked with Arabella toward the staircase, regarding her with concern.

"Did you hurt yourself much?" she inquired.

"I was a bit shaken up—but fortunately, I did not fall upon a tombstone."

"A tombstone?" Miss Derwyn echoed. "You were in the chapel grounds, then?"

"Yes, my horse bolted and threw me." Arabella flushed. "But you knew that."

"How did you happen upon the chapel?" Miss Derwyn inquired confusedly. "It is rather sequestered."

"I do not know—rather, you must pardon me, I do know—I was deep in thought—and not really looking where I was going, and all of a sudden, I was there—and well, you know the rest. Sir Francis also fell."

"Oh, dear, did he? He is not very familiar with the grounds either," Miss Derwyn said anxiously. "Where is he?"

Arabella shook her head. "I do not know. I thought him right behind me when I reached the edge of the grave-yard—he had guided me there, you see—but I was mistaken. And—" She stiffened as Sir Francis limped up the hall toward them, a bloodstained handkerchief wrapped about his head.

Staring at him in utter amazement, Arabella asked incredulously, "You—you have fallen again?"

He regarded her half dazedly, half angrily. "Where did you go?" he demanded.

"I—I was about to ask you the same question. You were right behind me in the graveyard."

"The—graveyard," he repeated confusedly. "I . . . have not been anywhere near the graveyard."

"But you were!" Arabella cried. "Do you not remember?"

"I was not in the graveyard, Lady Arabella," he said insistently.

"You appear to have hurt yourself, Sir Francis," Miss Derwyn said anxiously.

"It is nothing," he snapped.

"And you are very pale," Miss Derwyn continued, quite as if she had not heard his curt response. "I think it is best you rest."

"I expect I had better do so." He nodded and clapped his hand to his head. "Yes, I . . . will," he muttered, and with a half-angry, half-questioning glance at Arabella, he limped from the hall and started up the stairs.

"I vow!" Arabella cried. "He—he appeared angry with me—and before, he was so very solicitous. I wonder how he happened to hurt himself? He did not appear to be hurt when he showed me out of the graveyard, but I did earlier see his horse dash off riderless. Oh, dear, it is all very confusing."

"It does seem as if Sir Francis sustained a fall," Miss Derwyn commented.

"Not while he was with me. But, perhaps—no, he did not wear the bandage while we were in the graveyard. His fall must have happened later," Arabella said.

For some reason, Miss Derwyn released a long sigh. "Perhaps it did. Certainly, it would account for his confusion."

"His confusion—yes," Arabella said, feeling some confusion herself. She was very tired and her head was throbbing. She needed to lie down. She also needed to know why Sir Francis had told a deliberate lie.

One explanation did occur to her. Perhaps he had fallen twice, and struck his head the second time. That would account for his disappearance in the graveyard. Had he slipped behind one of the tombstones as they walked together, and she failed to observe him? There had been no bandage and no blood on his forehead nor on any other part of him when she'd seen him last.

"Might I help you to your chamber?" Miss Derwyn asked.

"No, I do thank you, but I am able to walk without assistance," Arabella assured her, wanting nothing so much as to be alone so that she might concentrate upon the events of the past hour and try to make some sense out of them.

On starting up the stairs, Arabella found herself shakier than she'd expected, and also a trifle dizzy. She stopped just before the first landing, clutching the balustrade and taking deep breaths in an effort to combat the encroaching dizziness, caused, she guessed, as much by her state of mind as by her fall. Then, looking up the stairwell, she tensed. Was that Sir Francis, still making his own way up the stairs?

She thought she had caught a glimpse of him. However, as she stood there, listening for the sound of his footsteps, she heard nothing, and another glance convinced her that she must have been mistaken. With a sigh of pure exasperation, she went on up the stairs to the first floor, and after taking a few more deep breaths, she mounted the second flight, glad that her chamber was but a few paces from the head of the stairs, else in her present state, she might not have been able to reach it.

Then, as she entered her chamber, she sent a long look about the room, hoping that she had, indeed, come to the right spot. On seeing her cloak lying across a chair where she had left it earlier that morning, she caught it up, stroking the material, needing to feel the reality of it in a place of so much confusion.

Then, as she turned to take it to her wardrobe, she glimpsed herself in the long mirror standing beside it and gasped. Her habit was much soiled, and there was dirt on her hands and on her face, as well. Furthermore, she was beginning to experience various aches and pains, brought about, she was sure, by her fall. If she did not have a hot bath, she would soon be feeling even worse!

She stepped to the bellpull that would summon her abigail and gave it a strong tug, and then sank down in a nearby chair. She wished . . . but she was not sure what she was wishing . . . her mind was truly in a turmoil! Putting her head back against the cushions of the chair, she defensively closed her eyes.

Someone was calling her insistently. "Milady, milady."

Opening half-dazed eyes, Arabella found a maidservant standing before her. "Where is Meg?" she demanded in confusion. "She is gone, milady. I am Jenny."

"Jenny . . ." Arabella repeated, perplexed. Then memory returned. "Oh, yes, I am sorry—I have had a bit of a fall."

"Yes." The girl nodded, adding sympathetically, " 'Twas in the graveyard, I hear. Is there aught I can do, milady?"

Arabella sighed. "Yes. It has left me rather sore. I would like a bath."

" 'Twould be the best thing," Jenny said. "I'll have them bring up the hot water."

"Ah." Arabella emitted a long sigh. "That would be lovely, Jenny."

The bathtub was full of hot, scented, soapy water. Lifting her washcloth, Arabella scrubbed first one arm and then the other, and then just lay there luxuriating in the wet warmth that soothed both body and spirit. Soon she would call for Jenny to wrap her in a towel—but she was loath to leave the water.

"And I would be loath to see you go, love."

Tensing, Arabella glanced up quickly and met the smiling, appreciative gaze of Sir Francis Knollys. A scream escaped her and, sliding under the water, she stared about frantically as she searched for a towel.

"By all that's godly, what ails you?" Jenny said, hurrying into the chamber.

"H-he—there," Arabella said, pointing a shaking finger at the spot where Sir Francis had stood, but stood no longer. However, in the air about her, she seemed to hear an amused laugh and a murmured, "Discretion, 'tis said, is the better part of valor."

"Oooh, it must have been him for sure," Jenny breathed.

"Him . . . who?" Arabella gasped. Then her confusion dissipated. "Of course, Sir Francis. The *first* Sir Francis!" she snapped.

"Aye, poor lad." Jenny nodded. "And doesn't he make it hard on the help—appearing and disappearing, as he does, scaring the maids out of their wits. Of course, there's not a particle of harm in him or in any of the others, either."

"You know about the ghosts?"

"Aye, practically the moment I set foot inside the door, the maids were telling me about them and saying I'd better not stay if I was the sort who scared easily. But bless you, 'tis not the dead I fear. There's naught they can do to me. In my years of service, it's been the living that have given me trouble—hiding in a girl's room and popping out at her as she's saying her prayers and all. And the mistress hot after her and accusing her of leading the young master on—when most of the time 'tis quite the other way around, begging your pardon, your ladyship."

"Oh, dear, that's terrible. I had no idea—"

"I am sure not. The housekeeper'll not tell the real reason why a girl's been dismissed. 'Twill be the poor girl's fault—not that of the master or his son."

It occurred to Arabella that Jenny spoke very well. Though she had a rather rough accent, her speech was careful and, for the most part, grammatically correct. Obviously, she was hoping to better herself and eventually escape the pitfalls into which pretty servant girls could so easily tumble. Arabella winced slightly; obviously, Jenny had been speaking from experience rather than hearsay.

Arabella felt it incumbent upon her to say, "Well, you will not have any unfortunate experiences here, Jenny. As you have said—and as I ought to have remembered—the ghostly Sir Francis has had his wings clipped, as it were."

"Aye, that's a fact to be sure, poor lamb. He died before his time, I've been told, and never got all the mischief out of him."

"I am sure he would be grateful for your understanding," Arabella said as, rising from the tub, she quickly wrapped herself in the towel Jenny had as quickly proffered.

"Will you be dressing now?" the girl inquired.

"No, I think I shall rest a bit."

" 'Tis better that you do," Jenny agreed. "With such a time as you have had."

Once clad in her nightgown, Arabella, lying in bed, sent her mind back over the events of that hectic ride. In her interior vision was Sir Francis, or rather, the Sir Francis who had been so ungallant as he showed her out of the burying grounds. If she had not been so shaken by her fall, she must have noted his antique garments. Of course, the real Sir Francis was wearing that ridiculous coat of his grandfather's that James had pressed upon him, so she had some excuse for the mistake. The reason he had not helped her was all too plain. He could only do as he had done—lead her from the graveyard! As for his descendant—the second Sir Francis—he must have been thrown from his horse due to the appearance of his phantom ancestor and, consequently, he must think that she had willfully ignored his injuries and heartlessly left him to fend for himself!

"Oh, dear," she said, and sighed. "I must explain, else he will have every right to hold me in anathema!" A second sigh shook her as she envisioned the ramifications of this misunderstanding, predicated on the look he had given her when he came limping in, and again when he had left to go upstairs.

As Arabella closed her eyes, she did not believe that, given the turmoil in her mind, she would be able to rest—much less sleep! Much to her subsequent surprise, on opening her eyes again, Arabella found the sun still bright—but a glance at the handsome timepiece on the mantel informed her that it was close on five in the afternoon. Or was it morning? No, the sun *was* in the west, and she had slept the afternoon away—dreamlessly, too, a boon she appreciated in this place where dreams carried with them the lineaments of reality.

However, large in her mind was the misunderstanding generated by the first Sir Francis—one that should have been explained before now. Yet she could not regret the long sleep that had rendered her much more rested. It would be easier to proffer the required explanations now that she was herself again.

She grimaced. No doubt the second Sir Francis must believe her heartless and, as for his ancestor, the sooner he was exorcised, the better! The moment this thought crossed her mind, she gazed warily about, fearing that he might be in her chamber, his mind alert to her thoughts. Fortunately, she had a strong sense of being alone—one that remained with her when Jenny, in answer to her ring, came to help her dress for the evening.

A half hour later, clad in her new blue lutestring gown, Arabella wondered if she dared request Sir Francis to come and see her. She hastily decided against it. It would be best to wait until after dinner.

Her aunt Margaret had told her that gentlemen were generally in a better mood at such times, depending, of course, on the degree to which they had enjoyed the meal. Sir Francis, she recalled, was not a heavy eater, but she had a strong suspicion that, in this case, her aunt was right.

On coming down the stairs, she heard the beguiling sounds of a pianoforte and recognized the music as that of Beethoven, a composer she much admired. Furthermore, it was one of her favorites: the *Sonata Pathetique,* and played by a master! And who might that be? she wondered. Miss Derwyn? No, she was almost sure the touch was that of a man.

Entranced by the music, she followed it to a door on the latch and, opening it very quietly, allowing no more than a half-inch of aperture, she could see the piano and, beside it, Miss Derwyn. The companion was looking down at the musician, whose face Arabella could not see—but whom she nonetheless recognized as Sir Francis!

Miss Derwyn, Arabella noted, appeared rapt in his music, as well she might be. Arabella stifled a sigh; it was certainly not a time for explanations. Indeed, she decided, it was best she leave—but almost immediately, a servant arrived and, with an apology to Arabella, opened the door all the way and hurried into the chamber. Regrettably, the music stopped midphrase as the servant explained that Lady Knollys had sent for Miss Derwyn.

Arabella, entering the chamber, stepped aside hastily as Miss Derwyn hurried out, followed by the servant. Much to her subsequent chagrin, Sir Francis, rising, also started for the door.

"Please," she said hastily. "Please, Sir Francis, I must speak to you."

He came to a stop, saying pointedly, "Good evening, Lady Arabella."

"Good evening, Sir Francis." She sighed, remembering that they had decided upon a dropping of their respective titles. It was not a time to dwell on that! Hastily, she continued, "You must understand why I did not come to your aid when you fell. You see, I thought it was you in the graveyard. You had gone on ahead, I imagined. Indeed, I—I am not sure what happened."

"I see," he said thoughtfully. "Tell me—what did occur in the graveyard?"

He listened closely and silently as she explained the contretemps that took place after her fall from her horse. Then, as she ended her explanation, she had a most uncomfortable feeling that he would not believe her. Indeed, as she waited for his response, she found herself holding her breath.

He said slowly, "I am not surprised. Francis—the first Francis—appears to delight in causing confusion. I am glad you told me what happened. I was worried about you. You seemed to disappear so quickly. And I hope you will tell me that you received no harm from your fall."

"I did not. Oh, dear, you also fell, and *were* hurt."

"Not grievously," he said, smiling.

"I am glad of that. Upon my word I am much reminded of *A Midsummer Night's Dream*, where Oberon had such sport with those unfortunate couples."

"The first Sir Francis does seem to share the fairy king's proclivities," he agreed wryly. "I would think none of the ghosts here are well-disposed toward their living descendants. As they were in life, so they are in death, with perhaps the exception of our doughty duelists, who are little more than boys—boys slain before their time under the banner of a less than noble king."

"That is true—though Robin Hood did honor the first Richard."

"It is such myths as that which spur our soldiers to battle, else many would lay down their arms and 'beat their swords into ploughshares and their spears into pruning hooks.' "

"Yes," Arabella said softly. " 'Nation shall not lift up sword against nation, neither shall they learn war any more.' It is one of my favorite quotations."

"Mine, too, even though I have not always abided by it," he said a trifle ruefully.

Gazing up at him, Arabella was about to respond when she noticed the dark bruise at the side of his face. "Oh, were you much hurt when your horse threw you?"

"Not really," he assured her. "I am no stranger to such happenings. Canada is not like England—though savagery is not restricted to uncivilized countries alone. But, enough, let us not dwell on that, especially since the savagery here can be easily obliterated by an accomplished exorcist and our ghostly population dispatched to heaven or hell—whichever place receives them."

"Have you met such an exorcist?" Arabella asked.

"I believe I mentioned a man in Richmond—I have it in mind to call upon him tomorrow. I think he must have returned by then. And—" He paused as they heard the crystalline chimes of a clock. "Ah," he added, "enough of our ghostly crew—James will shortly be summoning us to dine. Come, let me escort you."

"I do thank you, Sir Francis." Arabella smiled up at him, thinking, as she did, that the first Sir Francis was nothing but a pale shadow of this vibrant man—thinking, too, that never again would she mistake one for the other. Several other thoughts followed, but, she decided with some embarrassment, it was still far too early in their acquaintance to consider them.

"The ghostly crew . . ." hissed Lady Helena, taking a nervous turn around the chamber just vacated by Sir Francis and Lady Arabella. The folds of the last gown she had worn swirled about her, and her eyes, much praised by the Court poets, flashed fire rather than glowing "with lambent flame," as one aspiring versifier had put it. "We might be mariners!" she snapped.

"On an inland sea, quite," Sir Francis nodded, "and in danger of shipwreck unless we scuttle them and their nefarious schemes for our departure."

There were murmurs from the jousting pair, who understood the ire of their distant relatives but who had long ago given up hope at being understood by their fellow spirits. Still, they, too, had absorbed the fell intentions of the current Sir Francis and had duly offered their broadswords in the service of their spectral descendants and were yet seething over the summary rejection of those fearsome blades.

Lady Blanche fingered a dagger and conveyed her wishes with the lift of an eyebrow and a singularly sinister smile. Her long, graceful hands were used to further express her wishes as she made a stabbing motion.

Sir Francis laughed, saying in French, "You might have been effective with your babes, my love, but to those who throng the castle now, you'd be naught but an ill wind. 'Tis a pity you failed to scotch the snake who grew into the heir."

"Never say so," Lady Helena reprimanded him. "Had she succeeded, you would not have enjoyed as much of your life as you were given."

" 'Tis true, my Helena, you were a lovely armful."

"And you, a lying varlet!" She glared at him. "All those empty assurances of undying love—"

"Enough," he rasped. "We are here to discuss our present, not our past. And if we do not wish to be dispatched to the icy flames of hell, we must needs find a way to dispatch, instead, our enemies. One has troubled us enough already, with his plans for our disposal." He grimaced. "And that youth who bears my face is, in truth, a savage."

"Aye." Lady Helena nodded. "Like unto the red Indians who are said to populate the shores of that place called America."

"Quite." Sir Francis nodded. "His very garments are

proof of that," he said with a shudder.

Lady Helena unexpectedly laughed. " 'Tis marvelous, the resemblance."

Sir Francis regarded her coldly. "I fail to see it," he snapped.

"Come, come, love, it can be of use to us—so do not waste time in refuting that which is a fact."

"C'est vrai," Lady Blanche said, and nodded. She spoke again in a torrent of antique French, only to receive baffled looks from Sir Francis and Lady Helena.

"She grows incomprehensible again," Sir Francis said, sighing.

"Does it matter?" Lady Helena shrugged. "She appears to have some inkling of what we are saying and is in accord with us. They must needs be dispatched, and soon. . . ." She used her hands to pantomime a motion of strangling for Lady Blanche's benefit.

A smiling Blanche nodded and happily duplicated that particular gesture.

"Alas, 'tis a worthy notion, but what can we do who may neither touch nor thrust?" Lady Helena sighed.

"There are ways, my love." Sir Francis smiled. "Now, heed me, all of you!" Haltingly, he repeated that injunction in French, causing Lacy Blanche to grimace and the two boys to shrug and look blank.

Notwithstanding their confusion, he continued, "We are menaced by this youth why bears some resemblance to myself."

"Your twin, indeed," Lady Helena said.

"Enough," he chided. "We are from our subject. This young man must not be permitted to bring his exorcist here. I have listened to the plans he detailed to his pretty little cousin."

"I do not think her pretty," Lady Helena snapped.

"Helena," Sir Francis said, frowning at her, "one is quite aware of what you think of all females with the exception of your radiant self. Now, pray, let me continue. This girl and her lover, this present Sir Francis, must be dispatched, and quickly."

"But how?" Lady Helena cried. "We are powerless; we can neither strangle nor stab, more's the pity."

"Aye, but we have a human accomplice. My Constance will do my bidding; of this I have no doubt. And . . ." He paused as Lady Helena and Lady Blanche, hearing the name, laughed derisively.

"Trust you to use a woman. 'Tis an old habit," Lady Helena commented wryly.

"Old habits are often the most effective," Sir Francis retorted coolly. "My Constance will not be amongst the living much longer, as I am sure you are aware. But while she retains her physical form, I need not tell you that she will do anything I ask of her. She has told me that she can hardly wait to hear death's summons—that we may, at last, be together."

"Poor, poor creature," Lady Helena said, glaring at him. " 'Tis understandable why you were not sent direct to hell. 'Twould not be hot enough for you, the pox take you. Your sweet talk sent me to the stables and brought me naught but a blade in my breast."

"Come, come, love," Sir Francis commented with a roguish wink. " That was not the blade that first impaled you, and we both found it monstrous pleasant while the diversion lasted."

"Come, come, you speak of trifles," Lady Blanche snapped in her archaic French. She added coldly, "Of nothing, you understand?"

She received a mischievous glance from Sir Francis. " 'Twas not quite nothing, my Blanche, and 'tis a pity we lived over two centuries apart—else you must needs have agreed with me, I know."

There were frustrated grumbles from the jousters, and Sir Francis, smiling at them, nodded. "Very well, let us continue. We are agreed, all of us, that my namesake and the chit for whom he seems to have developed a tendre must be summarily dispatched. Yes?"

"Aye." The ghostly chorus brought a smile to Sir Francis's lips.

"Good. We are in accord, which is as it should be—no

more of this private moaning over a past that can be neither eradicated nor changed. We should all have progressed beyond our separate sorrows. Now 'tis time we concentrated upon an exorcism not of ourselves, but of our enemies, who must needs be summarily eliminated." Gazing into the blank countenances of the two boys and Lady Blanche, he sighed slightly and made a twisting motion with his hands.

"What is . . . eliminate?" Lady Blanche questioned.

"Les enfants, ma vie," Sir Francis said.

"Ah!" Lady Blanche smiled, and pantomimed a dagger thrust.

"Mais non . . . 'twould seem to them like a vagrant breeze." Sir Francis changed to English, finding Lady Blanche's language too difficult for him to employ. "We cannot stab or thrust—they must be led to their doom in the bowels of the castle, wherein you perished, my Blanche, and still haunt, your screams and wails falling upon deaf ears. For once, you will be heard, my beautiful, and strike terror into the descendants of the babe you failed to strangle." He pantomimed a babe held in his arms and subsequently made a strangling motion.

"Ah," Lady Blanche nodded, "splendid!"

"Now let us plan—" Sir Francis began.

At this moment, Jenny, coming into the chamber, stopped short, staring at them. "Lord," she said, "the lot of you!"

In one shocked moment, they faded away as quickly as blown-out flames.

She laughed lightly. "You need not go because of me. I cannot do anything to you, nor can you harm me. 'Tisn't often that my sort can see you, but I was born with a caul—mayhap that might be the reason."

She strolled about the chamber and, picking up a silver dish, gazed at it interestedly. " 'Twould bring a good price, this would, but there's more than dishes in this castle, so I've heard and have hopes of finding." With a provocative smile, she walked out, closing the door softly behind her.

They looked after her curiously.

"She can both hear and see us," Lady Helena murmured.

"Aye, and she's a pretty piece. But what is going on in that little head?" Sir Francis mused. "Someone should follow her and see."

"And are you taking that task upon yourself?" Lady Helena demanded.

"Who knows the ins and outs of the castle better than myself?" he asked reasonably.

"Ah, Francis, my love," Lady Helena said, and sighed. " 'Twas a sad day when you were spitted on your brother's sword. If he had only waited another decade or two—"

" 'Tis not her beauty beckons me," he said virtuously. "I have an odd feeling. . . ."

Their laughter was quick and mocking and even the two brothers joined that chorus as a grinning Sir Francis, with a lewd gesture including the lot of them, walked blithely through a wall.

=== 7 ===

DR. WINTERBOURNE, THE renowned exorcist, had returned to Richmond, Sir Francis found out via a communication from that worthy. Unfortunately, two days of blustery, rainswept weather had left the roads so muddy that he had found it regrettably necessary to wait yet another day before setting out on a journey which would end, he hoped, in a most fruitful meeting.

Mounted on Jacques, he passed through some beautiful countryside that he hardly noticed—his mind being fixed on the forthcoming encounter. Indeed, used as he was to the wild wastes and vast empty stretches of his native land, the mixture of cultivation and rugged fells of Yorkshire made very little impression on him. Of course, on reaching the town, he could not quite ignore the noble ruins of the castle rising above it, but again, his mind's eyes were turned inward anticipating that happy moment when he could converse with Dr. Winterbourne and subsequently set a time when the man could come to remove that quintet of specters that roamed the castle far, far too freely!

He frowned, thinking particularly of Lady Blanche, slayer of her own children, a Medea manquée! She would be the first to be dispatched and second would be Sir Francis, whose features mirrored his own. Subsequently, the two young men who had followed Richard I, a monarch whose reputation for derring-do had been romantically exaggerated, would be sent to their eternal rest.

After them would go Lady Helena. On second thought, should not Sir Francis be sent packing first of all? His presence caused naught but confusion! He frowned more deeply, thinking about his startling resemblance to his profligate, several-times-removed uncle. He found it singularly disconcerting that facial characteristics could be so closely duplicated despite the passage of a century and a half!

He ran his hand through his hair and shook his head. Had he not, out of consideration for Jean, allowed his hair to remain unshorn, there would have been no such contretemps as had recently occurred and poor little Arabella would not have been plagued by their intrusive ancestor! But consideration for Jean was something that was an integral part of his life, absorbed with the life-saving milk he had absorbed from his wet nurse, Jean's half-breed mother. He had often wondered whether they were not half brothers, as well as foster brothers.

His thoughts returned to Arabella and he flushed. It was difficult not to think of her. She was quite extraordinarily beautiful and, from the first, he had found himself much attracted to her. Indeed, he had been strongly tempted to invade her chamber and . . . He winced, hoping that such temptations had been due to a brief possession by his lecherous ancestor. It were better not to think of even closer comparisons, namely his late father, Sir Edmund Knollys.

He frowned. The first Sir Francis's proclivities, though not his misfortune, had been transmitted to Sir Edmund. That worthy or, rather, unworthy, had eloped with the daughter of an earl. Pursued and caught by her infuriated brothers, he had fought and killed one of them in a duel, thus making a return from Canada, whence he had fled with his beautiful prize, impossible.

There, despite a fortune realized in furs, they had lived most unhappily. His mother, whom he remembered as bone thin, whining and deprived of both beauty and health after the four miscarriages that followed his own birth, had never ceased to bemoan the loss of England.

She had cordially loathed a country fit, she insisted, only for the horrid redskins that roamed its forests. He, himself, had earned her opprobrium by insisting that he loved it.

He loved it still, and longed for the unspoiled wilderness in which he had grown to manhood. He had been early inducted into the fur trade, and had helped rebuild the family fortune. Unfortunately, the wealth he presently enjoyed had come too late to send his unhappy mother back to England. She had died when he was seventeen, and his father, some five years later, had expired in the arms of one of his mistresses.

Sir Francis winced. The late Sir Edmund had been a worthy successor to the first Sir Francis. Even his death mirrored that of his lustful forebear. He had been slain by an enraged husband whose child possessed various physical features more characteristic of Sir Edmund than of his putative father.

Francis shrugged. In those days, he had been hard put to understand his father, but his glimpses of his ghostly ancestor had, in addition to startling him, also reminded him strongly of his late parent. Fortunately, the latter had never come back to harass his Canadian associates or his English kin with his phantom presence. It was Sir Francis I who had driven the present Sir Francis to propose the exorcism, and that specter's subsequent capers in and out of the castle had served only to strengthen his descendant's resolve.

"Oh, yes, yes, yes, yes, Sir Francis," Dr. Winterbourne said eagerly. "One would find it a great, great honor to exorcise your castle. One has heard of its ghostly population, and one is most eager to put them to flight. Such a pother as these disembodied entities will create! I wish, in fact, that I had not a previous appointment at Fotheringay Castle, two counties from here. Lord Fotheringay has complained of a pooka, but I am quite, quite sure that it is his disembodied grandfather, quite senile he was at the end of his life and full of nasty tricks—the which I am not at liberty to recount—suffice to say that I am very glad to have the honor of sending the old man on his way."

"When might you be able to oblige us?" Sir Francis demanded abruptly, liking nothing about his host. The man was an odd combination of the servile and the sententious—fawning and, at the same time, lauding his many accomplishments in his chosen field. He had, he averred, rid the chambers of castles, the stages of theaters, the reading rooms of libraries, and the cells of prisons of numerous and horrific spectral manifestations that he, alone, had dispatched after scores of others had failed.

Oddly, Sir Francis did not like to think of the castle ghosts being summarily routed by this man and subsequently relegated to a testimonial signed by himself. Yet, given these peripatetic presences, he had no choice but to make an appointment with the fulsome doctor—the latter having ascertained that he would be free within a fortnight's time.

Meeting Sir Francis at breakfast, the morning after his visit to the exorcist's home, Arabella barely managed to avoid showing her great relief at seeing him smiling across the table.

"Did you see him?" she asked.

"Yes." He nodded and sighed. "I cannot like him."

"Oh? Then he is not coming?"

"On the contrary, he will be here. His arrival depends upon how quickly he can drive away a pooka from Fotheringay Castle."

"And what might a pooka be?" she asked interestedly.

"I think it is some sort of spirit—like Puck, for instance, and quite mischievous. In this instance, it seems to have invaded an elderly man, but it is my opinion that the confusion of old age animates him, not some occupying entity."

"Ah," Arabella said, "then we can expect he will be here soon?"

"Within the fortnight," Sir Francis said, frowning

slightly. "It is a pity that I am not better acquainted with this district. I am sure there are others in this same profession who would be more to my liking."

"Well," Arabella said reasonably, "if he is proficient in his work, you do not need to like him."

"That is true; and he does seem to be proficient. Judging from the number of testimonials he showed me, he has dispatched quite a number of invading spirits."

"I wonder where they go after they leave," Arabella mused.

"I would imagine, to their much-postponed eternal rest."

"They certainly deserve it after all these years," Arabella commented.

"Quite," he agreed with muted satisfaction.

"May perdition seize him!" Lady Blanche cried indignantly, as, with Sir Francis, she floated over the dining table listening to his quick translation of the conversation beneath them. "Had I been able to strangle the babe at my breast they, neither of them, would be here!"

"If I have properly understood your villainous speech, my dear, neither would I. 'Twas a good life while it lasted; neither can I complain much at its aftermath."

"*Peste!*" Lady Blanche glared at him.

"Come with me, my love," he said easily in French. "'Tis important that we speak."

"It is very difficult to understand you," she snapped, and with a glare, Lady Blanche flounced through the ceiling, followed by a laughing Sir Francis.

Arabella frowned, "I—I had a strange feeling that the air was . . . troubled."

"I, too," Sir Francis commented. "And will be until our exorcist arrives."

"I do hope he won't be long coming," Arabella said.

"It will be soon," he assured her. "Meanwhile, might I hope that you will come riding with me this morning?"

"Oh, I should love that above all things," Arabella assured him, and was immediately regretful that she had expressed herself so frankly and, she feared, forcibly. "I—I mean—" she began.

"If you do not mean exactly what you just said, I shall be mightily disappointed," he commented, his gaze on her face.

"Well, I—I did," she admitted, since at this moment, she found it far beyond her capacity to dissemble.

"Good," he said, smiling. "There is so much here you've not yet seen and which I would like to show you."

"And much here they will soon wish they had not seen," Lady Helena said. She had arrived in time to hear the last of their conversation, and with a most unpleasant expression upon her lovely face, she, too, hurried through the ceiling.

The argument had lasted quite a while, due mainly to the fact that much of it needed to be translated to Lady Blanche in a French that, though it might resemble, did not really equate with her own ancient tongue. Still, she had picked up the gist of the conversation and, by her nods and the sinister look in her eyes, showed herself in complete agreement.

However, the decision Sir Francis had been in hopes of achieving at once, was yet forestalled. He faced his angry cohorts with as much calm as he, as impatient in death as he had been in life, could muster.

"Why not Constance?" he demanded for the third time. "I have told you—indeed, you have seen for yourselves, that she is mine to command!"

"You cannot be sure of that, dear Francis," Lady Helena snapped. "Despite the progress of her fatal malady, she is human still. And, as such, might side more easily with her own kind than you imagine."

"Not she!" Sir Francis exclaimed. "Time and time again has she professed her loyalty."

"For loyalty read love," Lady Helena said, glaring at him. "But she has yet to die and, until she does, I tell you her allegiance will not be to us."

"She has already demonstrated—" Sir Francis began.

"What does he say?" Lady Blanche demanded in French.

She was immediately echoed by the two young men, who had been blankly staring from Lady Helena to Sir Francis to Lady Blanche, their faces registering a ferocious annoyance. Unfortunately, their Norman French, their few phrases in ancient Arabic, and their even fewer words in Old English were not enough to help them achieve any understanding at all, and their speech was rendered incomprehensible to the other three—even though Sir Francis knew a few assorted words in Lady Blanche's more evolved tongue.

Lady Helena sighed. "I cannot think which is worse— their villainous Norman or her—"

"Enough." Sir Francis frowned. "I tell you, Constance can understand all. She is a scholar and has a marvelous command over ancient French, even Norman French. And she will do anything for me," he continued with a complacency that Lady Blanche and Lady Helena, despite their difficulties in communicating with each other, had no trouble understanding, their looks implying that they were in total agreement concerning his insufferable self-satisfaction.

"Like it or not," Sir Francis snapped, "Constance is the bridge between our two worlds and it is to her that I mean to apply. And within the hour, I shall!"

"The dungeons?" Constance repeated, her loving gaze on Sir Francis's face.

"Hast never been there, love?"

His voice was, in her ears, sufficiently loud—an augmented whisper, which she could clothe with sound. She looked into his concerned face—so handsome and, no matter how strong the resemblance, much superior in her eyes to the features of his descendant, the present Sir Francis. She had taken a strong dislike to the current bearer of the name, for reasons she knew to be ridiculous; that he was so vibrantly alive, while her Francis was condemned to wander or, rather, float through these halls—a mere shadow of his former self. Now, hearing for the first time the plans of the living heir, she was near to loathing him.

"Constance," Sir Francis prompted, "you've not answered me. You do not know the dungeons?"

"I have never been there, my dearest," she said.

"Then, 'tis best I show them to you, my beloved. Canst come with me now? The old woman sleeps."

"I can come," she said, suppressing an impending cough. She was feeling oddly weary—had felt so upon awakening, but as usual, the sight of Sir Francis acted as a restorative. From the first, her pity for this handsome man, whom she had seen initially striding down the hall and walking boldly through a wall, had exceeded her initial fear.

Though her copious reading of the family archives had acquainted her with the ignominious manner of his death, such was his charm that she had immediately been strongly attracted to him. Then he, who had blithely confessed that during his lifetime he had found one woman much like another, had, much to his own surprise, developed a strong affection for her. She was the first, he had often assured her, who had had only sympathy for his unfortunate plight.

Constance, despite her own blameless existence, had defiantly ignored the transgressions preventing him from partaking of the joys of heaven, and had, just as defiantly, fallen deeply in love with him.

As her illness had progressed, so had her love. At one time the thought of the death that had seized so many other members of her family in its icy clutches had terrified her. Now her only fear was that, through some mischance, she would not be allowed to join her love in death. As, to her mind, her transgressions had already lost her all hope of heaven, she comforted herself with the thought that such a miscarriage of justice was highly unlikely.

"You must take candles, love," he instructed, "and a tinderbox, too."

"I don't want to disturb her ladyship. I will fetch them from the dining room."

"Very well, but hurry."

She had fears that the housekeeper might accost her as she took the candles and the tinderbox from a drawer in the dining room. Fortunately, she was not observed, nor did she meet with anyone during her subsequent foray into that part of the castle where lay Arabella's chamber and the paneled wall across from it. Set into the center of each panel was a carved flower, a Scotch thistle perhaps. Try though she did, she could not even glimpse the outline of a door.

"But where might it be," she demanded confusedly when Sir Francis suddenly appeared beside her.

He smiled at her. "Be patient, my dearest love. You must twist this flower." He pointed to one carved blossom, set in the middle of a group of three squares, each decorated with a similar blossom which adorned the panel.

"Twist it?" she questioned, puzzled. "It looks as if it were set fast against the wood."

"It is not, I assure you, love, and pray make haste, I beg you."

Thus adjured, she obeyed and found that the flower moved beneath her fingers. In another moment, she was staring at a door that had swung open, revealing a stairway descending into darkness.

"A—a secret passage," she murmured. "Where might it lead?"

"Into the bowels of the castle, my love, where few have ventured since my damned brother, my father, and myself lay there while above us the marauding Puritans invaded and searched what they believed to be every nook and cranny of the castle. 'Twas touch and go for a matter of three days until those varlets ceased to hunt for us. Then, upon abandoning their search, they seized our castle as their fortress. Damn them, may they rot in hell for the hypocritical knaves they were! But their hypocrisy served us well, for 'twas while they, roistering over their supposed victory and ill-gotten gains, lay wrapped in drunken slumber, that our faithful steward, who had brought food to us in our dungeon fastness— the while proclaiming loudly his Roundhead sympathies— helped us to escape and sailed with us to France."

"Oh, how exciting!" Constance breathed.

"Less exciting than terrifying, my own. My brother and I were but seventeen and fifteen. You'd not think that after all we suffered together, 'twould have been he who dispatched me when he knew his bride had succumbed to the king's blandishments long before she came to me."

There was a bitterness and an unhappiness in his tone that Constance had never heard before. She longed to clasp him in her arms and soothe his pain away, and then sighed, regretting that she could say only, "How terrible for you, my love."

"Aye, and more terrible yet that my brother had the key to heaven and flew there immediately he drew his last breath. Had he been with me—but enough, my own, let us go. And I pray you, watch your step; the stairs are steep and winding."

The wavering light of her candle proved to Constance that the steps were not only steep, they were heavy with centuries of dust. And above them hung veritable curtains of cobwebs spun by generations of spiders, horrid filaments that brushed her face. She tried to push them away, biting down with some difficulty the exclamations of shock and disgust that threatened to escape from her.

Intermingled with those feelings was the memory of what Sir Francis had just told her. In her mind's eye, she could see the frightened youths crouching in their dark, dank hiding place that, for the moment, had become a prison, too; while above strode certain death in the persons of those joyless Puritan scoundrels.

Her vulnerable heart went out to him and, as usual, she excised from her mind his ignominious demise and also those wandering eyes that in the passage of a hundred and fifty-odd years had not ceased from gazing upon those whom he could no longer possess—a fate she suddenly knew to be quite as virulent as hell's eternal flames! A near stumble swiftly brought her mind back to the present.

"Beware, my dearest," came his whispered warning, "I'd not have you harm yourself." He sighed. "My arms were passing strong. 'Tis a pity I have not the use of them to hold you, my sweetest love."

"You are here, Francis, and that is enough," she murmured.

"Had you lived when I lived, my beautiful, we'd have shared heaven together."

"You have made me feel as if I shared it now," she assured him.

"Ah, my love—but enough, we are finally at the bottom of the stairs. Your taper is flickering. Quickly—light another from its dying flame."

"I shall," she replied at once and, while doing so, stared curiously about her at the towering walls that rose to form a vault high above them, again festooned with the webs of generations of spiders. To her left, she saw that the walls curved and formed a wide passage into which Sir Francis moved.

"Follow me," he said. "Hold your light on high."

In doing as he commanded, Constance wished she could not see the texture of the wall through his transparent form. But, she ruefully reminded herself, it had always been thus and she had never loved him the less because he was without substance.

Hard on that thought, he turned, his ardent eyes visible in the flickering flame of her candle. "My very dearest, how could I love you more than I do? You are, in truth, too good for the likes of one whom even hell would not receive. Unless I say in the words of Christopher Marlowe's earth-visiting demon, 'Why, this is Hell nor am I out of it.' But surely that cannot be so. Not when you gaze upon me with your sweet eyes and teach me love; I who had never known its full meaning until now. But enough! I must not allow myself to be diverted.

"Once our persecutors are through the door in the

paneling, which you will have left ajar—a temptation neither will resist—they will walk boldly into the darkness. When they have reached the point just ahead, where the passage branches—the timing of this is vital—their candles will be extinguished and, above, the door closed against their return. We shall do the rest."

"What will you do?" she breathed.

"Very little, love. Once they are here, they will effect their—er—departure from the castle by themselves and none shall be the wiser. Their cries for help will be as lost as they themselves." He paused and then added, "I believe you shuddered, Constance."

She had been unable to help it, but, at his comment, she said quickly, "No, Francis, love, I assure you I did not. It is a proper fate for them."

"Ah, my beautiful, I had hoped you would agree. Now come, I will lead you forth into a larger light than is shed by this candle, here. Only, I charge you, keep in mind the path they must follow."

"I already have it marked," she assured him.

The stairs leading up to the secret door were much steeper than Constance recalled. However, she reminded herself that a descent could not be compared to an ascent and, despite her encroaching weariness and a nagging pain in her chest, she was pleased that the plans of the second Sir Francis and little Lady Arabella would be foiled. In common with the first to bear the name of Francis, she was quite sure that once they were blundering through the darkness below, they would never find the stairs—much less the door, which she would have closed against them.

Look like the innocent flower, but be the serpent under it. Constance grimaced as that advice of Lady Macbeth came into her mind. She feared she could liken herself to that evil lady and for very much the same reason—the advancement of the man she loved or, in this instance, the saving of his fragmented existence and that of his companions, too.

Her thoughts were driven out of her mind as she continued to ascend the stairs. Despite her joy and relief at the impending rout of Sir Francis's distant descendants or, rather, relations, she was quite dreadfully weary, and cough after cough racked her as she slowly made her way to the door.

"You must rest, my love." His soundless admonition echoed in her mind. " 'Tis a pity you dwell on the third floor. I beg you to take the stairs slowly—very slowly."

"I do not mind," she whispered, wincing as she always did whenever she saw the blood-edged tear in his coat where his brother's weapon had dispatched him as he lay. . . . But she would not dwell on that guilty coupling.

Finally, finally they were at the entrance to the passage. The door swung open at her slight push, and they came forth into the light. At his hasty reminder, she left the secret door slightly on the latch, so that a faint line of darkness attested to its presence.

"Now come to your chamber, love," he urged. "You must needs rest."

"Aye, I must," she breathed, and was immediately sorry she had acknowledged her weariness. It would trouble him, she thought as she went down the hall and turned into the passageway that led to Lady Knollys's chambers and also to the stairs up to her own.

She was even more spent when they reached her door. The chill wind that swirled about her, which she knew to be his embrace, conversely heated her blood and made her long for that closer union that would come with death.

He accompanied her into her chamber and waited while she gratefully lay down upon her bed. Then his lips, alas unfelt, were on her mouth.

"Rest, love, rest—and remember that before this day is out, our enemies will be gone." He moved away.

"Where do you go?" she asked plaintively. "Will you not remain with me, Francis?"

"I shall return when you are more rested, my sweet love," he murmured. "And by then—they will be gone." He smiled.

She tried to smile back at him, but could not manage it, as her mind furnished pictures of that hapless pair who would, who *must,* be lured to the dungeons. "Is there no chance they—they could be merely frightened away, not starved to death, as they will be?" she asked.

He frowned. "Is your heart faint within your breast, then? Would you fail me, too, Constance?"

She could not resist the pleading in his voice, could not bear the thought that her failure to assist him would result in his departure—thrust into oblivion by the man who, irony of ironies, bore his name and in whose veins ran the blood of their common ancestors. She said, "No, I promise that I will do as you wish, Francis."

"Ah, my love." He blew a kiss at her and vanished more quickly than she liked. She closed her eyes against encroaching weariness and wished she could sleep until it was time to go to dinner. Sleeping, she would not be able to dwell on the pending fate of little Arabella and Sir Francis Knollys. She found herself wishing that he had remained in Canada—and Arabella in London. Fate, unfortunately, had intervened, and who was she to contend with Fate?

Her eyelids were so heavy . . . Constance came to with a start, realizing she had allowed herself to drowse off. Worried lest she miss Arabella and Sir Francis, she quickly descended her staircase and peered into the corridor just in time to see them disappear through the door in the paneling. She waited until she judged they would be past the curve in the passage, then crept out and firmly closed the door. It slipped from her grasp and closed with a bang that seemed to her to reverberate through the castle like the Crack of Doom.

=== 8 ===

A LETTER TO her father being long overdue, Arabella was seated at the charming little desk in her sitting room, writing it. She was telling him all about the castle, but she had decided not to mention the resident specters. Some cronies of her father had once told him of a haunted house in the precincts of London and had been much put out by his derisive laughter. Indeed, one of them had been more than half inclined to challenge him to a duel for doubting his veracity and also for that same mocking laughter. That had not come to pass, but a coldness yet remained.

She could envision his reaction were she to describe the entities thronging the castle! Consequently, she contented herself with describing the grounds and some of the chambers. She would have preferred to fill that same letter with her description of, and her feelings for, Sir Francis, but discretion in this case was certainly the better part of valor. Her father was quite aware of the age of Lady Knollys and her inability to act as a chaperon. Naturally, he would accuse Arabella of dalliance. Writing finis to her letter, she signed it affectionately.

Coming out of her chamber with the intention of taking her letter downstairs where it would be collected and posted, she sighed. A glance from her window had showed her no improvement in the weather. She had been told it rained a great deal in the North, and obviously that was true, even in summer. She felt rather ill-used, then chided herself for being ridiculous. The weather was the weather, and one could not accuse it of deliberately filling the sky with scurrying rain clouds.

Then, suddenly, she came to a startled stop as, directly in front of her, she saw the outlines of a door where no such thing had ever been before!

The portion of the wall facing her was similar to the rest of the wall all along the corridor. It was divided into squares, and each square had in its center a carved and gilded flower. There were three squares a panel, and this particular panel was slightly open so that the lineaments of a door were clearly discernible. Another glance showed her that were it closed, it would indeed present the appearance of a solid section of wall!

Moving closer to the panel, she tentatively pressed her fingers into the crack, which subsequently widened slightly. Arabella, managing to grasp the edge of the panel, pulled it back. It moved with surprising ease. Looking into the dark aperture, Arabella saw steps—leading where?

Her first impulse was to descend those same stairs immediately! This particular notion was replaced by a second impulse informing her that it was very dark beyond that door and would grow darker still, the farther she moved away from the hall. She would have to fetch candles from her chamber.

She turned back to do so, but came to an abrupt stop. It had occurred to her that she did not really want to venture into that passage alone.

Should she summon a servant? No, the logical person to accompany her was the master of the castle—Sir Francis Knollys. Where might he be found? she pondered. Of course, the library!

At breakfast, he had asked her if she wished to go riding. She had joyfully voiced her acquiescence at the precise moment a rumble of thunder smote their ears. It was followed by a blinding flash of lightning and another clap of thunder. He had gazed at her ruefully, saying, "I think our ride must wait. Perhaps I will explore the library instead."

"And I must needs write to Papa," she had said.

Now, tentatively, she approached the panel again and placed her hand on its edge. She pushed it forward. It moved easily. Leaving it nearly shut, she hurried down the stairs and, seconds later, left her letter on a table in the lower hall. Then, coming up to the first floor, she walked though the portrait gallery into the library, hoping to find Sir Francis. A hasty glance around the vast chamber showed her that he was, indeed, still there, seated at a table, an ancient volume open before him. He appeared to be deeply engrossed in his reading, and she wondered if she ought to disturb him. Perhaps later . . .

Then, as she hesitated, he looked up and smiled warmly. "Ah, good afternoon, Arabella," he said cordially. Before she had a chance to return his salutation, he continued. "Can you imagine what I have found? It is a Gutenberg Bible—printed more than three centuries ago."

"Oh, really." Arabella tried to sound as enthusiastic as Sir Francis, even though she was not quite sure what a Gutenberg Bible was. But she would not ask him—in addition to displaying an ignorance he might find disappointing, the panel was large in her mind. Excitedly, she said, "The panel, Sir Francis, it—"

Before she could explain further, he looked at her questioningly. "The . . . panel?"

"A door—a secret door—across from my chamber. It is open."

"A secret door?" he repeated.

Arabella hastily described the appearance of the wall, adding, "I pray you will come and see it for yourself. But first, we will need candles."

"And a tinderbox," he said, nodding. "But are you sure?"

"You must see it for yourself," she urged. "Please come now."

A glance at Sir Francis's face showed Arabella that he was quite as interested as she. The failure of the brief storm earlier to clear the sky of its clouds, and the continued threat of rain, had been disappointing to them both. However, the idea of exploring a secret passage—at least she assumed it was secret since no one had mentioned it to her—was fascinating! Indeed, her excitement was increasing by the moment, and she resented even the brief time it took Sir Francis to request candles from the housekeeper.

He brought them into the library, quoting what he described as the housekeeper's acid-edged comments on the fact that there had been no candles to be found where she had first directed a footman to look—in the drawer of a chest in the dining room. She had spoken darkly about "things disappearin', quite as if they'd walked off by themselves." She had also given it as her opinion that it was "a mercy they'd had a recent dipping, else they must have been sadly candle-poor." She had also adjured him to be careful with the flint.

"You did that well," Arabella said, laughing at his mimicry. "You could easily be an actor."

"I thank you, milady," he said, bowing slightly. "It is a profession I admire. Traveling actors are most welcome in our wild Canadian provinces."

"And have you seen our English actors?" she asked. "There is a theater in Richmond."

"We must attend a performance," he said, smiling, "after I am properly outfitted, else I might be mistaken for a member of the cast."

"Since most of the actors I have seen in London are extremely handsome, you might." She smiled, then blushed, belatedly realizing that her comment bordered on the bold. "I mean—" she began confusedly.

"I hope, as I said before," he interrupted, "that you mean exactly what you just said, my dear cousin."

She met his dark, slightly amused gaze and blushed again. "Well, I—I did," she assured him. "Come," she added, "do let us explore the passageway."

"I am yours to command," he said, grinning.

She had not closed the tiny crack that had led her to the secret panel, lest she could not find the place again.

Now she worried lest a passing servant should have closed it. That fear was alleviated as they reached the panel in question and found that narrow line of darkness running the length of the cream-colored wooden wall.

Exchanging excited glances and, with wary looks in both directions, they stepped to the panel. Though Arabella longed to pull it open, she stood back as Sir Francis slid his finger along the crack, pressing against it.

He gave a surprised exclamation as it swung back easily, exposing a flight of narrow steps progressing downward into the darkness.

"Oh, lovely," Arabella whispered. "I wonder if Aunt Juliana is aware of this."

"There is no telling, but it does seem to me that if she had had any knowledge of it, she'd have passed it on to me. She has been most informative about the castle. She has, I believe, hopes that I will make it my home."

"And is that what you intend?" Arabella asked.

He hesitated. "I've not come to any decision as yet. I have another home—near York in Canada."

"But you've no need to return," Arabella said quickly. "All of this belongs to you."

"And my house in Canada also belongs to me. . . ." He paused, then went on. "But enough, let us go down into the—er—bowels of the earth and see what we may discover." He laughed. "God knows what we may find."

As she stared into the darkness, Arabella was suddenly conscious of cold shivers coursing up and down her back. It was on the tip of her tongue to protest this descent. Yet why? It certainly promised excitement.

One of her favorite books, *Lady Carlton's Coffin,* came to mind. The plot told of finding a strange sarcophagus hidden in a secret passageway in an ancient castle much like this one, and guarded by the ghost of an Egyptian pharaoh. The heroine had suffered many vicissitudes before escaping from that same passage, she remembered.

Arabella felt a frisson of fear pass through her. There were ghosts here too. Where did they dwell? Once more she was conscious of an urge to turn back, but Sir Francis had pushed open the door and had stepped carefully down on the first of those winding stairs. And she must follow, else he would think her a coward, which she was not!

As they carefully picked their way down in the flickering light of the candles, both commented upon the shrouds of cobwebs. They agreed that these appeared willfully torn, suggesting that someone else had used this same staircase recently.

"Who?" Arabella wondered aloud, and then became a little angry at his suggestion that it might have been she.

"I swear it was not," she cried hotly. "Upon my honor, it was not."

He laughed softly. "Hold, my dear, I do believe you. And I am glad you did not attempt the descent alone. These dusty stairs are both narrow and treacherous. It is fortunate we have our candles."

"Yes, indeed," she said as she followed him along the wide, curving passage. She could see in the fitful flicker of Sir Francis's candle that just ahead the passage appeared to branch in three or four directions.

Glancing back over her shoulder, Arabella realized that the curve of the passage now hid the spill of light that had previously outlined the door. Seized by another shiver of fear, she said, "I think it might have been better had we told someone of our intent."

"That would have taken most of the spice from the adventure. Still, you may be right," he acknowledged ruefully.

"I think—" she began, and came to a startled stop at the loud slam of a door. She bit down a scream of terror.

"Good Lord!" Sir Francis exclaimed. "Who was it shut the door?"

"I—I do not know. A—a servant, perhaps," Arabella faltered.

"The devil take them!—and myself, too. I should have seen to it that somebody knew our whereabouts. We must go back up, I am afraid."

"Yes, I do agree. These candles shed very little light and—oh!" she cried as the flame of her candle flickered and went out—as if someone had blown upon it. A second later, Sir Francis's candle was as hastily extinguished and the impenetrable darkness enveloped them.

Even as he had drifted to the upper levels after extinguishing Sir Francis's and Arabella's candles, he had felt the girl's presence. She had climbed to the walk stretching between the two towers, the one containing Constance's chamber, the other vacant. What was she doing there? Had she no garments to mend, nor to iron, nor a chamber to tidy?

Yet, why dwell on the reasons for her presence on that half-walled walk? No, she was no longer there, his well-honed senses informed him. She had entered that empty tower and stood near a window, staring out. He was reminded of the *Morte d'Arthur,* with its tales of captive maidens rescued by King Arthur's knights.

These had thrilled him as a lad, making him long for the days of old. It was a pity that only the two young brothers, of all the knights who had thronged the first castle, remained. Had they been evil enough to fall directly into the fiery pits of hell, or good enough to be wafted straight to heaven? Lady Blanche had known those of the later era; he could ask her.

No, she remained concentrated on only one of them, he whom she had killed while he lay sleeping—but yet had had a son to carry on his name. Again, he could not decry that.

His thoughts fled as he saw the girl stepping from the tower entrance and onto the narrow walk between. She moved swiftly and then stopped, leaning against the parapet and staring down, while the wind swirled her skirts about her and tousled her golden curls. She was a pretty piece, to be sure, and he would very much like to know her better—and that wish being father to the thought, he moved to her side.

She glanced up at him and, without a trace of fear, she said, "Ah, there you are. Certain sure, you must have bedded your share of lasses in your time."

He was startled by her bold address and also by her lack of fear, but both, he thought, were most intriguing. And even more intriguing were her actions since arriving at the castle. Intent on ascertaining the reasons behind them, he set out to charm her. Her lovely little face and her small but perfectly formed body made that task no hardship for him.

"How do you know me?" he asked.

"Haven't I seen your likeness in the portrait gallery?" She shook her head and sighed. " 'Tis a great shame that most of you is missing."

"Not all, fair maid." He smiled.

"Aye," she said, nodding solemnly. "There be enough of you to make me wish I might feel the rest."

"Ah, and I am sure you are a sweet armful, and have been so to many!"

She drew herself up. "You be a bold one, for sure. If you had a solid cheek to slap, you'd be for it."

"Alas, you make me wish I had—but also you set me to wondering why such a canny little lass as yourself is lingering in this lonely castle."

"Lonely for some, but not for others." She winked. "I'd lay a monkey that you do not want for company and have not these two hundred years or more. How many lassies have you bedded in your time, laddie? For sure, you'll tell me you've lost count."

"Alas," he said, pretending to sigh. "You can ask me that, and yet see the shape that I am in?"

"Shape or lack of it, you've found ways to pleasure yourself, I'll be bound, laddie. Indeed, I'd lay a guinea on it."

"And I, my beautiful, would lay—"

She emitted a trill of laughter. "For shame, Sir Francis," she said, shaking a finger at him.

"Not for shame, fair maid, but for pleasure."

Staring at them from her window, Constance, her heart still beating heavily in her throat from her climb and tears coursing down her cheeks, turned away. Their windborne words had been wafted into her ears—she could always hear him and, of course, had no trouble hearing the girl's pert answers as she boldly teased and flirted with him, whose eyes remained on her alone.

Meanwhile, she shivered, thinking of Lady Arabella and the man who so closely resembled Sir Francis and bore his name as well, but who had inherited little of his easy charm and, perhaps fortunately for him, nothing of his character. It was he whom Francis would leave to starve in company with that poor young girl, who, after all, was quite blameless!

She shuddered, remembering how easily she had acquiesced to her Francis's nefarious plans. But he was not *her* Francis. He belonged only to himself. Angrily, she blinked her tears away and wiped her cheeks. Hastily picking up the candles and tinderbox again, she hurried from her chamber.

Candles in hand, she had an uncomfortable spell of dizziness and needed to lean against an adjacent wall until it passed. She felt uncommonly light-headed, and a spasm of coughing shook her. As usual, she brought her handkerchief to her mouth to suppress it, and as usual this was unsuccessful. As usual she found bloodstains upon it when the paroxysm ended, and she removed it from her lips.

She sighed, unwillingly remembering her mother in her last illness—such stains had been on her handkerchief then, and she had hastily hidden them away, so as not to frighten her little daughter.

"You are a good child, my love," the dying woman had murmured. "But I know what ails me, and I pray you escape it . . . such a lovely girl you are . . . you do not deserve such a fate."

"Deserve . . ." Constance murmured, glad her mother slept deeply in her grave and could not know the path her daughter had taken—nor the man, whose charm had so beguiled her that she had willfully ignored the precepts learned in childhood. For that sin she was paying heavily—so heavily . . . so heavily.

Sir Francis's light laughter had filled her ears as he jested with the little maidservant, who had blithely given him jest for jest—looking upon him with knowing, mirthful eyes, inviting those caresses she could not feel.

"I've been three kinds of a fool," Constance whispered to herself. "But my foolishness is at an end." She looked down at the candles, glad that she still had a large supply. She would need them, and so would the hapless victims of those wayward spirits. Somewhere a clock chimed twelve. She would soon be due in Lady Knollys's chamber; she hoped her ladyship would forgive her absence—but of course she would, even if she were given no reason for it. She was uncommonly kind, tolerant of the living and the dead.

Another cough shook her, and she hastily pressed her handkerchief to her mouth. Then, knowing what she would find once she took it away, she merely thrust it in her sash and, despite the weakness that had occasioned her retiring to her chamber, she continued on her way— to free the last of the Knollys family from Sir Francis's sorry vengeance.

On arriving in the hall, she could see no sign of the secret door, but she clearly remembered its location. Putting her hand to the flower on the middle panel, she twisted it as she had at Sir Francis's instructions and smiled with relief as it moved beneath her fingers.

In another moment, the door had swung back and, clutching her candles, Constance left it carefully on the latch. Lighting a candle, she started down the stairs, her ears attuned to every sound—such as frightened sobbing or a cry for help.

Finally, she reached the bottom and saw the same wide passage she had noted earlier. The floor was coated with centuries of dust, but in places that dust was disturbed by two sets of footprints—one large, one small.

She wanted to call out, but dared not do so in case there were ghostly ears attuned to her. She shuddered. She had never feared them before—but now that she had become their enemy, what might they not do?

Nothing, her common sense told her. It was part of their punishment that they were powerless to harm the living—at least those who did not possess weak hearts or weak heads. They could, of course, lead them astray and abandon them to their fate. One needed to remember that they were only shadows—even Sir Francis was a shadow. Why, why, *why* had she given ear to his blandishments, he who was condemned—as were the others—to forgo the joys of heaven?

She tensed. She heard voices, and not far away. She turned toward the sound and noticed a passageway to her left and again heard a cry.

"What is it, love?" she heard a man, Sir Francis of course, ask solicitously.

"I felt . . . Oh, God, where are we that none can hear us call?"

"I do not know where we might have blundered—I felt a door and hoped . . . But, alas, I was wrong. I beg you will forgive me for this curst venture."

"It was I who instigated it, and I am the one *you* must forgive."

His tone was comforting as he replied, "Let us absolve each other of blame and concentrate on finding a way out, my dear. We seem to have come to a room of some sort. I will try the tinderbox once more. I am certain it is possible; after all, many blind people do similar tasks all the time.

Constance received the impression that Sir Francis was still firmly in control—an admirable control, considering their desperate situation. Arabella, too, appeared determined not to yield to a useless hysteria.

She had earlier disliked and resented both of them—but now she felt a strong surge of shame. She had been instrumental in their plight and, had she not had second thoughts, must have been a party to their probable demise—a horrid death, starving in these dark corridors where, in centuries gone by, many a wretched prisoner . . . She shuddered and, following the direction of their voices, came upon a cavernous chamber where, to

112

her horror, was a rack and a pile of dusty ropes upon the floor. A noose dangled from the ceiling and, in a corner, there was a gaping space in the wall where, possibly, a panel had yielded to their frantic pounding. At the same time that these images were impressed on her mind, she was conscious of cries of relief.

"A light, Francis, a light—"

"I see it. Come."

From the darkness of that vast chamber, Sir Francis and a trembling Arabella came forward.

"Miss Derwyn . . ." Arabella cried unbelievingly. "Oh, how did you know? Oh, thank God, thank God!"

Sir Francis came toward her, too, and Constance winced as she saw his face—a replica of the man she had betrayed. But had he not betrayed her, leading her into folly as he had so many foolish females—until he died for it? And had she not heard him laughing with the maid, she might have left these two young people to their horrid fate!

"How did you find us?" Arabella asked in quavering tones as she stood in the circle of Sir Francis's protective arm.

"I will explain later, once we are safely out of this place." She held out her candle to Sir Francis, who lit his own from it.

"My thanks," he said. "Ours blew out."

"I do not know quite how, but it was as if a—a strong wind blew them out," said Arabella. Then, looking about her, she shuddered. "Where are we? There—there's a noose dangling from the—the ceiling and, over there . . ." She gazed at a high bench with ropes at either end.

"That would be a rack," Sir Francis said grimly. He suddenly paused and then added, "But what is that, over there, on the shelf?"

Looking in the direction he indicated, Constance saw the splintered remains of a panel that must have been broken in their blind efforts to escape. Behind it lay a large box, or rather, a small chest with a rounded top. From its imperfectly closed lid dangled a string of pearls that caught the gleam of the candle and glowed like so many small moons.

"The treasure," Constance breathed. "The lost treasure!"

"The treasure?" Sir Francis questioned.

"It disappeared, so Lady Knollys told me, centuries ago," Constance said.

"My father told me about it!" Arabella exclaimed. "He said it was buried—somewhere in the castle."

"It is as good as buried here," Sir Francis commented, a muted excitement edging his tones.

"Lift it down, Sir Francis," Constance said. "And be careful. It might be heavy."

"May we hope that it is," he said, and handed his candle to Arabella. With a grin he removed the chest from the shelf, adding, "It is quite heavy." No sooner than he made this observation, the flames of the candles flickered for a moment, then burned strongly again.

"Oh, God—there's no breath of air down here," Arabella cried. "It must be . . ."

"I beg you'll not be afraid," Constance said calmly, "but I think we should go."

"Yes," Sir Francis agreed, a trifle grimly. "It is hard indeed to realize that malevolence can last beyond the grave."

"They are not malevolent!" Constance exclaimed. "They are frightened only."

"Frightened? *They?*" he questioned incredulously.

"The living pose a threat to the dead," Constance told him coolly, "particularly when they are determined upon exorcism."

"But—" Sir Francis began, and paused as he felt the frenzied pressure of Arabella's fingers on his arm and guessed its import. With a visible effort, he abandoned the argument and said, "Will you please show us the way back?"

"Yes, I have come to lead you there," Constance said, nodding.

"It is most kind of you. Let us be on our way, I beg you," he urged. "And let us hurry if we may," Sir Francis added. "This chest grows heavier by the moment."

"Is it too heavy for you to carry?" Arabella asked.

"No, I can manage it," he assured her. "But it would be best to take it with us. I have a feeling . . ."

"Yes. It is much better to remove it at this time," Constance agreed. "And—and we must go. It is passing close in here and dusty."

"Yes, indeed it is," Sir Francis said. "Please show us the way."

Nodding, Constance moved out of the chamber, easily finding the corridor leading to the stairs. "There," she murmured, feeling very weary. "I beg you'll both go ahead of me. I must take the stairs very slowly."

"Perhaps you should rest here," Sir Francis said. "It is a steep climb, and I'll return to help you once Arabella and the chest are safe above."

Constance watched them go, then, uneasy waiting alone, began to climb. It was even steeper than she had remembered. She was rendered breathless even before she had negotiated five of the many steps she must needs climb to reach the door. And she was feeling so very strange, so spent, and even more breathless.

In fact, she had a strong desire to sit down and, after mounting two more steps, she could not resist that particular temptation. Sinking down, she leaned back, feeling incredibly weak. Indeed, it was even difficult to draw a breath.

She had always suffered from shortness of breath—but never, never so badly as now. Closing her eyes, she rested her forehead upon her knees and a slight moan escaped her. It was followed by another as she wondered what Sir Francis, *her* Sir Francis, would think of her. Would he hate her for her interference in his schemes? Would all of them hate her?

"Never think so, my very dearest," he said. "We have no blame for you, who did only what you thought was right. And 'twas right. I should not have burdened you with this, and I should have been at your side ere now, my beautiful."

Looking up into that handsome, that beloved face so

near her own, Constance sighed and said, "But I have betrayed you, Francis."

"No, my love," he said soothingly. His arm was about her shoulders, and suddenly the troubling image of Jenny near the towers was forgotten as, for the first time, she felt his strength and gloried in that feeling even though she did not understand it.

"You will, my dearest," he said, kissing her. She felt that, too, a tingling through her whole body down to her very toes! Putting her arms around his neck, she rejoiced because, through some miracle she could not comprehend, he was no longer a shadow. He was substance, warm and vibrant. Then those thoughts were swept from her mind as she thrilled to his passionate embrace.

They had reached the top of the stairs and, much to Arabella's relief, a thin line of light from the hall indicated that the door was again ajar. She thrust it farther back and hurried into the corridor, turning to hold the portal open for Sir Francis, who passed through it and gratefully put down the chest.

He wiped his hands and glanced back down the stairs. "I must return for Constance." He turned and went slowly back down into the darkness. A few minutes later, Arabella heard him give a sharp exclamation.

"What is the matter?" she called. "Did she fall?"

"No . . . I will bring her up," he said.

Arabella pulled the door open all the way as Sir Francis returned, bearing Constance in his arms. "Did she faint?" Arabella asked, concerned.

"We'd best take her into your chamber," he said huskily. "Come."

Arabella hurried to open her sitting-room door and then pushed open the connecting door to her bedchamber. "You'd best bring her in here," she said as he followed her into the chamber. He obeyed, putting Constance gently on the bed.

Arabella said, "Poor thing—she does look so pale. I'll fetch my hartshorn."

"There's no need," he said huskily. "She has ceased to breathe, Arabella."

"Oh, no," Arabella said. "You—you'll never tell me so." She stared down at Constance's face, surprised by the slight smile on the woman's lips. She looked uncommonly beautiful, but she lay so still—everything about her was still . . . still . . . still. Arabella bit down a sob that was insisting on rising and said, as calmly as she was able, "I will fetch Jenny. Rather, I shall ring for her."

"Yes, and I shall need to tell my grandmother." Sir Francis paused, then added, "But first I'd best bring the chest inside."

"The chest? Oh, I was near to forgetting that," Arabella said.

"As was I." He went back into the hall. In a moment, he returned, frowning. "It's not there," he rasped.

"Not there?" she echoed. "But it must be." She would have run into the hall had he not caught her arm.

"It is not there," he repeated. "Someone has taken it."

She regarded him blankly, her mind full of questions that she could not consider now—not with poor Constance dead and the news yet to be broken gently to Lady Knollys and the others in the house.

Quite as if he had read her mind, Sir Francis nodded. "No, the treasure is no longer our first priority. We must needs inform the staff of Miss Derwyn's death. But first, I think, we must go to my grandmother—before she hears the news from others who may not know how to break it to her."

"Yes," Arabella said. "Let us go at once, then—" A sob escaped her. "But I hate to leave Miss Derwyn here alone. . . ."

Sir Francis looked at Constance's face—lovely in its last sleep—and at the smile that yet curled her lips. "I wonder if—if she *is* quite alone," he said. And, feeling a tear in his eye, he turned swiftly away, adding huskily, "Come, my dear, we must go to my grandmother."

=== 9 ===

SHE WAS NEARLY winded when she reached her miserable little room on the fourth floor, which was the servants' floor. The rest of that lot enjoyed larger chambers. The housekeeper had a bedroom *and* a sitting room, if you please! She, the latest addition to the staff, had been given what was little more than an attic!

However, as she pulled open her door, Jenny was not displeased at her room's location. It was at the end of a very long corridor and not sandwiched in between two other rooms as a lot of them were. She needed privacy now, and must needs invent some excuse as to why she was unable to answer Lady Arabella's bell if, indeed, it rang, which it had not—as yet.

She set the small, heavy chest on the bed, not trusting the spindly, splintered legs of her table to bear its weight—it *was* weighty. And what else besides those milk-white beauties lay in the depths she had not yet explored? Obviously, there would be similar or even more costly treasures!

It was fortunate, indeed, that she had happened upon that open door. There had never been a door there to see before! It was even more fortunate that she, hearing voices coming from the darkness beyond that portal, had used her much-praised presence of mind to dart into one of those empty chambers on that same side of the corridor and peer through a minute aperture of its door in time to see Sir Francis bring an unconscious Miss Derwyn through that strange door and across the hall into Lady Arabella's chamber.

It was then she had glimpsed the chest and the string of milk-white pearls dangling from it—magnificent pearls! The chest was dusty, very dusty, as if it had lain forgotten for years and years—centuries, even!

No one had ever said that little Jenny was not quick to seize an opportunity or anything else she could safely steal. She had dashed out, caught up the chest, and, even though shocked by its weight, she had managed to stagger back into that empty chamber and quietly close the door. Subsequently, she had progressed though three other empty chambers to the point where the steps to her floor lay.

She was still panting with the exertion of carrying the chest all that way and up those narrow stairs and down the corridor to her own chamber, praying all the while that she would meet no one—and she had had a large serving of her usual luck, God or devil sent! Once more, she whispered a thanks to whichever entity was appropriate for the brains meted out to her. From the age of five, she had been called a "knowin' un." And knowing she certainly was. She had a nose for it, she did, and hadn't she proved that in all the places she had worked?

Her clever thefts had always been blamed on other foolish servant girls. No one had ever put the finger on little Jenny. And no one ever would—because once she and her accomplices had split the loot in this chest they would vanish from the country, at least for a while, and who knows, one day she might become "her ladyship."

Meanwhile, she must not sit about daydreaming. The lads would be getting mighty impatient waiting for her signal—she imagined that the necessity of avoiding the keepers was getting on their nerves. To her mind, this was the ideal time for them to make their move! The companion had obviously bought it, and Jenny could finally give that signal that would bring Alf and the others hotfoot to the castle this very night, and the grieving inhabitants none the wiser! No doubt Lady Arabella and

Sir Francis would be in Lady Knollys's chamber giving her a lot of unfelt condolences over that redheaded witch's untimely death.

"Untimely?" Jenny murmured gleefully. "It couldn't have happened at a better time—not if I had arranged it myself. . . ."

Unaware of curious eyes upon her, Jenny quitted her chamber and hurried along the corridor bound for the walk between the two towers adjacent to the companion's room. She hummed a little tune as she went. As one of her mistresses had been fond of quoting, "all's well that ends well." And the end she had in mind could be very well, indeed.

She was truly weary of all the shifts she had had to make in the last few years, weary of serving young women who were no better than herself and not half so clever. Now, at last, her years of service for very little remuneration would be recompensed, and she would be able to give orders rather than receive them.

She wished she did not need the boys to help carry away that chest. She could envision the contents—pearls, rubies, diamonds in heavy gold settings, and would she not look like a queen with those pearls around her neck?

Unfortunately, it was share and share alike and the boys would be eager to sell the lot and collect the profits—unless she could think of a clever way to cheat them.

But that was something to consider later, not now. She had overheard Lady Arabella and Sir Francis discussing breaking the news to Lady Knollys. No doubt they had gone to her by now, and the old crone would be in a rare taking. The shock might even kill her—which would be all to the good, for, of course, it would leave the castle in even more of an uproar!

Meanwhile, Jenny thought she had better be about her business. Lady Arabella might be calling at any moment, and she had best be in hearing distance—so it was time and past that she got to the tower to signal the boys.

She was extremely pleased to find that the castle corridors were empty of the maids and other servants who usually busied themselves with various chores. No doubt they were all gathered in the kitchen, or maybe in the housekeeper's quarters, discussing the demise of Miss Derwyn.

But it hardly mattered where they were. There was no one about, and emerging onto the narrow walk between the towers, Jenny leaned over the parapet and waved the scarlet scarf that had summoned her confederates into many another household—be it castle or mansion.

Four times she raised and lowered it, which meant they must invade the castle that night. She smiled as, in the distance, she saw the brief emergence of another scarlet cloth. They were on the alert—they had seen and would act at once, with the setting of the sun.

Jenny smiled happily and thrust the scarf into the bosom of her dress. She was glad the period of waiting was finally at an end. With an impish little grin, she kissed her hand to the tower at her side. She would be leaving the castle soon, considerably richer than when she had entered it. And perhaps, after all, she would find the means to retain some of those lovely gems for herself!

"And shall this wretched wench, this double-dealing doxy, no better than she should be, put her greedy little claws on the treasure of the castle?" Lady Helena demanded rhetorically. "To my thinking, she ought to be broken on the wheel or, better yet, burned at the stake!"

She directed her statements to Lady Blanche, who, in common with herself, stood near Jenny—carefully out of the girl's range of vision, since the miserable creature could, as she had proved to Sir Francis, see them all too well! Then, meeting Lady Blanche's habitual blank yet baleful stare, she crossly indicated the door behind the girl. Fortunately, Lady Blanche caught her meaning and, moving through that portal, was swiftly followed by Lady Helena.

"*Nous avons besoin,* Sir François," Lady Helena said.

"*François, oui.*" Lady Blanche nodded.

Well, at least she understood that, Lady Helena thought crossly. But she strongly suspected that her other comments had been incomprehensible to one whose French had been learned some four hundred years ago and whose English remained willfully unlearned.

Still, she had probably understood the import of the signals that wretched little chit had been making. She was also sure that Lady Blanche had seen the scarlet cloth in the distance, emerging from the green leaves of a tree and being waved up and down three times. As these suppositions coursed through Lady Helena's mind, Lady Blanche whirled on her, speaking rapidly.

Lady Helena had never had more than a rudimentary command of the French language—she had not needed to! She had a superb ability in the unwritten language of dalliance, and this, combined with a few words gleaned from various lovers come with Charles II from the French court, had sufficed. But Lady Blanche's pronunciation was not the same, and the few familiar words Helena did catch brought to mind a necklace in which various beads were missing, giving the whole a horrid lopsided look!

She hastily abandoned the analogy and tried vainly to catch even a word or two. She did hear the name "Jenny," and a gesture or two made toward the distant trees caused her to believe that Lady Blanche had, indeed, seen that scarlet cloth seemingly growing on a branch.

She said, *"Il n'est pas un fruit dans cette arbre."*

Another flood of French acknowledged her comment, and with it were head-shakings and hand-shakings as well. Indeed, it appeared to Lady Helena that the usually cold, composed Lady Blanche was endeavoring to speak with her whole body! As usual, it was impossible to catch her meaning, and again, as usual, Lady Helena was miserably positive that, despite the location, she and her fellow specters were lodged in some anteroom of hell.

"But you are not, my dear, and nor am I. I have never experienced hell and I have a strong feeling that, at this moment, I am close to paradise."

Sir Francis, looking younger and happier than Lady Helena ever remembered—not even when first she met him and knew immediately the sport she might anticipate on those occasions when her husband was conferring with his tenants. She smiled at him, her eyes filled with memories that fled as soon as she saw the young woman at his side. Jealousy rose and fell as she breathed, "Miss Derwyn!"

"Lady Helena, I bid you good afternoon," Constance said equably. In another moment, she went on in a peculiar French that Lady Blanche, staring at her incredulously, answered in those same cadences, smiling more broadly than Lady Helena remembered her doing in the hundred and fifty-odd years of their acquaintance.

Had she Constance Derwyn's supreme command of languages old and new, Lady Blanche could have told Lady Helena that she had just been addressed in the tongue she had spoken upon arrival at the castle, and to which she had clung despite numerous angry attempts at coercion by the terrible man who had taken her as a spoil of war.

She would never forget his striding into her chamber, where her young and much beloved husband, Yves, lay wounded. The conqueror had regarded her out of wide, smiling eyes and kissed his hand to her. Then, turning on her husband, he had savagely gutted him as one might a new-caught fish!

If she still had had tears to shed, she would have had to let them fall for the memories Constance's words conjured up. Yet she was grateful for having heard them—to the point that a veritable torrent of words poured forth, expressing for the first time that never-forgotten anguish. Then, finally, abruptly, she ended an outburst deeply shocking to one who had kept these festering thoughts to herself for centuries.

Half defiantly, half furiously, she faced Constance, cursing her for her willful use of that ancient tongue, but whatever she had anticipated in the way of a like response failed to come. Instead, Constance, disengaging herself from her lover's arms, moved to Lady Blanche and put an arm around her rigid shoulders, murmuring gentle words of sympathy, not blame for those crimes that kept her earthbound.

She received an incredulous stare from Lady Blanche, who loosed another stream of discourse. Again Constance replied and received a beatific smile, the first Lady Helena and Sir Francis remembered seeing upon Lady Blanche's lovely but usually dour countenance.

In another moment she had seemingly asked a question, and again Constance answered and smiled, replying in that peculiar French. Then, for the benefit of the two others present, she added, "Lady Blanche wishes to learn English, and I am sure I shall be able to instruct her—now that I have the time."

"The time . . ." Lady Helena repeated as she and Sir Francis exchanged rueful looks.

"Yes," Sir Francis said. "You will have the time, my love, but you must not use all of it in teaching."

"Oh, I shall not, for I will be learning, too." Constance gazed at him with her heart in her eyes.

She received an equally loving look. "And I, my beloved, shall be your most fortunate teacher," he said.

"But, meanwhile, what of this Jenny, who has in her greedy little hands the treasure of the castle?" Lady Blanche demanded.

"We shall need to see that she does not retain that treasure," Constance answered in that antique tongue. "I had an uneasy feeling about her—a pity I did not act upon it." She hastily translated their comments into English for the benefit of Lady Helena and Sir Francis.

"And now," Lady Helena said, frowning, "her accomplices will scale the castle walls come sundown."

"We must be waiting for them," Sir Francis said grimly.

"But what can we do?" Lady Helena demanded.

"You must appeal to your great-nephew," Constance said.

A chorus of indignant negations poured forth from the lips of Sir Francis, Lady Helena, and even Lady Blanche, who had gathered some inkling of the import of Constance's reply.

"He would have us broiling on the spits of hell," Sir Francis cried.

"I think," Constance said calmly, "that he may be made to change his mind—and meanwhile we cannot let those miscreants with their thieving fingers take what has remained in the family for centuries."

"No, you are right," Lady Helena cried.

Constance hastily translated the import of her speech for the benefit of Lady Blanche, who also nodded her acquiescence, adding in French, "They should be stretched on the rack or, better yet, boiled in oil!"

"Where are the lads?" Sir Francis suddenly said. "We will need them. But how may we communicate? We who have no knowledge of their villainous speech."

"I will speak to them," Constance said, smiling at him. "We have met on the stairs from time to time and exchanged a few words."

"Is she not a treasure?" Sir Francis asked lovingly.

"The real treasure of the castle, to be sure," Lady Helena agreed with a generosity uncommon to one who, until this moment, had had scant liking for the female gender.

"It grows late. Look, it is nearly dark," Sir Francis said. "It is time we approached my—er—nephew, and perhaps . . . the little Arabella."

Lady Helena glared at him. "What can she do, that child?"

"We might need her *human* hands once those miscreants are subdued. You forget that we are powerless to *touch* the living," Sir Francis reminded her.

"Alas," Lady Helena sighed. "That is the truth. Best alert them now."

He thought, as he first entered, that he was looking at his image in a mirror—but the mirror in his chamber did not face the door. After the first startled glance, Sir Francis noticed that the man facing him wore a ruffled shirt and trousers of a dark maroon that were gathered at the knees and fell from hip to calf. Furthermore, the coat was a bright yellow with ribbons at the shoulders. He had seen similar costumes in paintings and knew them to be worn by the men of fashion who thronged the court of Charles II.

"Quite right, Nephew," the visitor commented in tones that whispered and sighed like an echo, falling into silence. The man's eyes, dark brown like his own, were fixed on his face as he continued. "You are not attuned to my voice, but I think my words do not go quite unheard. And I see that your eye strays to the blade in my heart—let its position trouble you not. The wound ceased to pain me minutes after 'twas received. I wore the weapon only to prove my identity, and will remove it now." Quite casually, Sir Francis drew the poignard out.

"See. 'Tis further proof that I am but an image, but though I am sure my plight must shock and surprise you, I am quite used to it by now. Also, I am quite used to this castle and would be loath to be sent to some unfamiliar shore—be it higher or lower. However, I've not come to argue my case, but rather to warn you that the time is fast approaching when we must needs engage and, I hope, defeat our common enemies."

Regarding his visitor calmly, Sir Francis said, "You are my uncle, many times removed, I believe."

"Aye, your uncle only, for I sowed no seed that took root in the proper soil—for all you are my mirror image as to physiognomy. To return to the point, I come, as the Greeks, bearing gifts of a nature that must needs prove disturbing, and I wish I might do more than merely prate about the forces who intend harm here."

"Harm?" Sir Francis echoed.

"Aye, a doughty trio of rogues and their doxy, who serves the little Arabella. The wench has purloined the casket of treasure and imagines there's none who know 'tis in her chamber."

"Jenny?" Sir Francis questioned incredulously.

"Aye, the same. Her fellow rapscallions number three. They are already within the castle, and tonight will make their escape with their booty. They must needs be stopped, and for that we depend on you. We have no choice." Sir Francis sighed as he added, "I admit freely that we did decoy you to the dungeons. 'Twas out of anger that you'd send us we know not where for all we are quite harmless. I know that you will contradict me as you recall how you were decoyed below, but enough. Those who have stolen the treasure are here, and though we shall aid you to rout them, 'tis your hand must needs wield the weapon. I pray you will be in agreement with me, rather with *us*."

Listening to this extraordinary discourse, Sir Francis, somewhat against his will, found himself pitying the handsome man through whom he could see the vague outlines of the chair behind him.

It had taken considerable bravery for the ghostly Sir Francis to approach one who he must know had been determined to send him from the castle—forth into hell or limbo—but Sir Francis II remembered from perusing the family archives that, rogue or not, Sir Francis I had never been wanting in bravery and had fought valiantly for his king on the latter's meeting with a paid assassin bent on murdering him. For the first time, he found himself critical of the brother who had dispatched him.

"I am glad you have some . . . understanding of me," the ghostly Sir Francis commented. "Is it not strange that we two—so far apart in years—should wear the same face? Yet I cannot imagine the confusion will last long, for you are bound to Canada once more."

Sir Francis tensed, regarding the spirit incredulously. "How do you know that?"

" 'Tis a part of the transition we have undergone. We have so little left to us. . . ." There was regret in Sir Francis's eyes, and it colored his speech as well as he continued with a slight shrug of the shoulders. "But we *are* uncommon knowing, and I have come to put this knowledge at your disposal. Will you have it?"

"Please, I should be exceedingly grateful," Sir Francis said warmly.

"Then let me suggest a device that must confound them. They seek to ransack the castle of more than the treasure for the nonce in Jenny's keeping. My senses inform me that they are not averse to murder and might wantonly slay Lady Knollys and Lady Arabella, too, for the girl Jenny envies her and might see her dispatched for no other reason than her burning jealousy. So, I charge you—believe that we will do what we may—and, as for you, lock little Arabella in her chamber and lock, too, the doors of Lady Knollys's room."

"I shall," Sir Francis promised. "And—" But he spoke to air, for, with a smile, his many-times great-uncle had vanished. But in his ear was the lingering whisper, "I shall be back—in time."

Out of force of habit, the depressed cook prepared an elegant dinner that was to be served at the surprisingly late hour of nine, but gave it as her honest opinion to an equally depressed staff that she did not see as how anybody would be able to eat a morsel of that repast.

Though there was a chorus of agreement from the kitchen staff, that kind lady, deep in depression, failed to see the hopeful looks exchanged by that same staff. These good folks were sorry about Miss Derwyn's unexpected death, but, at the same time, they looked forward hopefully to the more-than-ample remains of a dinner composed of a fine soup, roast lamb, an excellent assortment of vegetables, and a dessert that, from the looks of it, promised to be food for the Gods!

"Nine. It be uncommon late for dinner," Jenny said as she assisted Arabella to dress for the meal.

Arabella regarded her with a slight smile that, she hoped, hid her burgeoning rage at the duplicity of her thieving maidservant, Sir Francis having informed her of his enlightening conversation with his uncle. She said, "I expect it is because it grows dark so late up here at this time of the year—York is considerably farther north than London. I understand that in Sweden, Denmark, and Norway the sun shines at midnight in the summer."

"At midnight." Jenny shuddered. "Oooh, that be mighty queer. I wonder when they go to bed?"

"I hear that they remain up all the night, because in the winter it is dark most of the day."

"I—I shouldn't think that anybody'd want to stay up all the night," Jenny commented.

Arabella heard anxiety in Jenny's tone and quite longed to inform her that she intended to stay up past midnight herself. But that might alarm the chit, and it might prevent her from putting her fell plan into action, and the sooner she and her comrades were routed, the better it would be. Consequently, Arabella emitted a long sigh and said, "I, myself, am uncommonly weary. I intend to retire for the night immediately upon finishing dinner. It has been such a terrible day, with poor Constance dead!"

"Aye, 'tis terrible indeed. She was a nice lady, that's a fact," Jenny said. "Her ladyship must be that cast down."

"She is, of course," Arabella said, sighing.

Jenny nodded. "I expect she'll feel better in a day or so. It be a sad shock for her, no doubt."

"Yes, indeed it has been," Arabella agreed.

"There—" Jenny slipped the last tiny button into its minute hole. "You be done, milady." She flushed. "I mean . . . dressed."

"Your meaning was entirely clear, Jenny." Arabella bestowed a warm false smile on her maid. She rose and glanced into the mirror. "You do have a way with hair, Jenny."

"I thank you, milady." Jenny bobbed a curtsy.

"I hope, in fact, that you will come to London with me when I return, Jenny."

"Oh, I should love that, milady, though I'm promised to another post come autumn," Jenny said with an equally warm, equally false smile and another curtsy.

As soon as Arabella had hurried down the corridor, Jenny dashed up the stairs to the fourth floor and down the corridor to one of many unused chambers. In earlier years, these had been allotted to one or another member

of a larger staff than that which now served the household. Now, they offered the perfect concealment for her
partners in crime. She tapped three times on the door,
which was opened so hastily that she was nearly catapulted inside.

"Oh," she said crossly, "will you look out how you—"
She broke off. "Enough! I've bad news for you."

"Bad news?" Two burly men and a smaller, shorter
individual moved to her side, their heavy-featured faces
reflecting a communal frown. "Wot news be that?" a
pockmarked man demanded.

"They'll be having supper at nine, Bert, and will probably be at it until long past ten." Jenny sighed.

"Dang 'em," muttered another man, known as Pudge,
by reason of his large accumulation of weight. "Why not
scrag 'em all now 'n' 'ave an end to it?"

"Aye, that's just like you," Jenny said, frowning. "Act
first and think afterward."

"I'll 'ave you know—" Pudge began angrily.

"Stow yer gab," snapped the third of the trio, Alf. He
was a thin, nervous young man with a face like a weasel,
but his eyes were bright with intelligence. " 'Er Majesty
here's never been wrong yet. We'll wait 'til she give us
the signal, cullies."

"And wot'll be the signal? 'Ave ye thought o' that one
yet, ducks?" Pudge growled.

"Aye, I'll knock on this door three times."

"An' won't they be wonderin' at that?"

"No one will hear. Little Lady Arabella'll be off to bed
immediately dinner's over. She told me that she's ever so
tired and upset about Miss Derwyn's death."

"You're sure you din't 'ave an 'and in that?" Pudge
asked.

"No, 'twas natural. She was sick as a dog, spitting up
blood all the time."

"An' wot about Sir Francis?" Alf asked.

Jenny shrugged. "If he sees or hears us, he'll be one
against three."

"And the servants?"

"They have themselves a drink every night after they've supped. 'Tis the best wine in the cellars, 'n' I know the bottle. When they down it this night, 'twill be tomorrow morning before they wake up," Jenny said with considerable satisfaction.

"It do seem mighty strange to me that them two 'aven't 'ad themselves a look for the missin' treasure chest," Pudge said, frowning.

" 'Twas Miss Derwyn's dying put it out of their minds, I am sure," Jenny said, smiling.

"And you say *you* didn't 'ave an 'and in that?" Alf gave her a suspicious look.

"On my honor, I did not!" Jenny said solemnly.

"Best you swear by somethin' else," Bert muttered.

"I'll have you know—" Jenny began angrily.

"Stow it," Alf commanded. "We'll be 'avin' ourselves a fine dustup, if we're not careful."

"Aye," Pudge nodded. "But the devil take this long wait!"

"It won't be for nothing," Jenny said.

"Yes, my Jenny, you be a treasure for sure," Pudge said.

"Aye, that be true enough." Bert grinned. He raised his glass. " 'Ere's to our Jenny. An' may'ap we'll be down in the kitchen 'n' 'avin' ourselves a fine meal afore long."

"Aye, you will, or my name's not Jenny Stowe," she said, smiling.

" 'Tisn't the name you gave 'em 'ere," Pudge said.

" 'Twill do for them." Jenny shrugged.

"No, 'tis us'll do for 'em," Alf said with a leer.

Bert, on the other hand, scowled. "Damn this long wait," he muttered.

"My signal'll come quicker than you think," Jenny assured him calmly.

"I am to stay in Lady Knollys's chamber with the door locked!" Arabella said in a low, furious tone of voice as she faced Sir Francis across the dining table.

"I am told," he responded with a patience he was far from feeling, "that the thieves are already here, in the

131

castle. My informant was not sure of their location. I have been warned that both you and my great-grandmother are in great danger. Since I cannot be in two places at once, and since we are certainly in for trouble, this seems the only way to protect you both. Furthermore, without Constance at her side, Lady Knollys is particularly vulnerable."

"Oh, dear," Arabella said, giving him a shamefaced look. "I had not thought of that. So very much has happened. Poor, poor Constance. Aunt Juliana seems to be taking it wonderfully bravely."

"Yes," he said. "The servants have been so helpful, too. Now, listen to me; you are remaining with her for your mutual protection. If anything untoward does happen, can you use a pistol?"

"Yes, I have bested Papa at target practice on many an occasion," Arabella said, adding resentfully, "I could be very useful to you."

"I am counting on the fact that you will be even more useful where you will be staying. Remember, we need you to reassure my great-grandmother." A sigh escaped him. "I do not know what she will do without Miss Derwyn." He shook his head. "It must have been a sad shock."

"Yes, she depended on her for so much. Poor Constance, and poor Aunt Juliana, too. I must visit her more often."

"I, too," he said ruefully, "but . . ." He paused as the servants brought in the main course of their dinner.

"Oh, dear," Arabella said, and sighed. "I am sure I shall not be able to eat."

"And I assure you that you must eat, if only to give yourself strength for what will happen. We *are* in danger, my dear cousin. There's no gainsaying that."

Despite her own uneasy feelings, Arabella wished that Sir Francis had not addressed her as "cousin." It put a distance between them and chilled the warmth she had been experiencing even in these moments of approaching peril. However, she said merely, "I will keep that in mind, Cousin Francis."

=10=

THE CASTLE WAS satisfyingly dark and still. In various chambers, clocks, silently or with chimes, had more or less accurately marked the hour of midnight. The sun had long since lost even a streak of vermilion across the western horizon. Its sister, moon, alone, shed its chill light in the darkened sky.

In her chamber, Lady Knollys slept, happily dreaming of running across the palace floors with her best friend, Sarah Lennox, and the young prince, George, who flirted with them one moment and made horrendous faces at them the next!

" 'Tis as dead as a doornail—the castle," Jenny said happily. "As I told you—the servants are dead asleep in their chairs. However, as I also told you, this place is haunted and you're not to take fright should you see one or another of *them* roaming the castle corridors. Some people can see them, others can't. Or perhaps *they* can make themselves be seen when they fancy.

"Now, pay attention to me. In addition to the treasure, there's gold and silver plate downstairs. 'Twill bring a pretty penny, and the lot of us can live like ladies and gentlemen on the proceeds."

"Talk about sow's ears," Alf said, laughing.

He received a glare from Jenny. "On what we pull in from this night's haul, we'll all be silk purses for sure, and we'll never need to lift a finger in any sort of work— and we can buy ourselves a fine house and—"

"If we scrag them wot lives in this one, we could stay 'ere," Bert said, grinning.

"Aye," Pudge agreed. "I'm for scraggin' the lot o' 'em, save for that young'un I caught sight of. She be a right pretty little piece."

"None of that, or you'll find yourself kicking the clouds," Jenny warned. "We will get the silver and all else we can carry, though we have most of that already in this box. 'Tis real heavy. When we're out of here, we'll see what's inside—a king's ransom, I'll be bound."

"Are you sayin' ye've pried it open a-ready?" Bert said, glaring at her. " 'Aply you 'ave yerself a few sparklers. 'Tis share 'n' share alike, remember?"

"Aye, thass a fact," growled the other two men.

"I've taken nothing," Jenny said, glaring back at them. " 'Tis locked, and God knows where the key is. 'Twill need to be broken open once we're away. Now, in the butler's pantry, there's the silver—plates and tankards and eating utensils! There are also bowls and ornaments for the tables. 'Twill fetch a good price, the lot of it." She paused as the chimes of the clock sounded the hour of twelve and a quarter. "Ah." Jenny's eyes gleamed. "There—mind you move slowly on the stairs, for there are some of them that creak."

"You ain't talkin' to no jobbernowls," Pudge growled. "Us knows wot to do."

"Aye, thass a fact," Bert said.

"You will please remember what I told you. If you have eyes to see them—you'll be able to recognize all five of the ghosts."

"We be none o' us afeared o' ghosts," Pudge growled.

" 'Appen there'll be others joinin' them ghosts afore this night is over," Alf said, grinning.

"Not unless 'tis necessary." Jenny frowned. "I've told you and told you 'tis best to draw the line at murder. Now, let us go, and be quiet about it—and do not become scared by what you see or, rather, think you see."

As the foursome slipped out of the chamber and

started down the hall, Jenny in the lead, the silence that prevailed in the castle was all-encompassing to the point that their very footfalls sounded incredibly loud. In a sharp whisper, Jenny ordered them to remove their shoes. Seeing the wisdom of that advice, they stopped to do so and then continued on down the stairs, their goal being the castle's fine array of silver.

As they reached the middle of that long staircase, they were suddenly confronted with the sight of the youthful pair of jousting ghosts—fiercely flying at each other with their mighty broadswords gleaming as they engaged and withdrew. Then one, slightly taller than the other, sliced his opponent through the body while the "wounded" lad retaliated with a stroke to the neck that must have decapitated his attacker, were he mortal. However, his victim's head remained securely on his shoulders and he, turning toward his pursuing brother, hit him squarely in the chest—the point of the weapon subsequently protruding from his back. Then both lads, swords extended, rushed toward those descending the stairs.

With a yell, Pudge, who was the closest to the lethal-minded pair, screamed in utter terror, rushing forward only to stumble and fall upon the stairs. The duelists, swords extended, leaped upon him.

Not heeding Jenny's cry that he was in no danger, Pudge rose and dashed down the stairs, with the duelists keeping pace on either side of him. With a scream, he missed his footing on the polished stairs and fell, rolling down that long flight of steps to lie very still at the bottom.

"God rot him," Jenny spat. "They can hurt no one! They've been dead for hundreds of years."

" 'E be dead, too," Bert said in quavering tones. "Look at the way 'e's lyin'—still as a corpse."

"Aye," Alf muttered. "I'm not going any farther."

"God rot you, too, for a pigeon-hearted gaby," Jenny snarled. "Watch me!" she said, and ran lightly down the stairs, walking through the young men impotently menacing her with their mighty phantom broadswords. Gazing over her shoulder at her comrades, she snapped, "See—they can hurt no one. They've been dead these six hundred years or more."

She had been determined not to let him face the villians on his own. So once she had ascertained that her great-great-aunt was deeply asleep—thanks to the laudanum drops Ellen, her maid, had insisted she take—Arabella had not stayed to sit with her. Instead she had crept out, carefully locking the door, and had tucked the key into the bodice of her gown.

It had been at this moment that a sudden realization had shaken Arabella—she had forgotten to arm herself with her pistol! What use would she be to Sir Francis without that? As swiftly and as silently as she had been able, Arabella had run back to her bedchamber.

Now, alarmed by Pudge's scream, she moved hastily toward the door and stepped over the threshold—onto an old board, which in the manner of its kind, let out a creak, that echoed round the stairwell.

"What's that?" Jenny whispered, glancing upward. "Ah, I know."

Arabella hastily groped for the door to her chamber, just as Jenny, rushing up the stairs, saw her outlined in a spill of moonlight.

In a trice, she reached Arabella's side, catching her by the arm in a hard, hurtful grip. "Well, as I live, 'tis her little ladyship," she hissed.

"Let me go, you thieving—" Arabella began loudly, only to be silenced by Jenny's hand over her mouth. At the same time, she was seized by Alf, who grinned down at her.

As Jenny backed away, Arabella opened her mouth to scream. But the sound was quickly choked off by her new captor's hard hand.

"Be silent, dearie," he muttered, "else y'll 'ave my dagger between yer ribs, 'n' that'd be a sad end. For y'er a fetching little wench, if the moonlight don't deceive me."

136

He turned to Jenny. "We'll have to take this chit with us."

"That you bloody well won't," she snapped. "No further than out the door and leave her body amongst the trees. I'd kill her here save that we might lose our footing, slipping on her blood."

"We'll talk about it later, love," Alf said.

Shuddering at this sinister exchange, Arabella realized how careless she had been. She didn't even have her pistol, which she'd risked so much to get. However, it was possible that she could still alert Sir Francis to her plight. But where was he? She would not dwell on that now—she must needs seize the moment, if, indeed, one should occur. She prayed it might and, subsequently, it seemed as if those prayers were answered, for Alf's hand had momentarily relaxed.

"Let me go!" Arabella screamed loudly. She was vaguely aware of a fist descending and then knew no more.

"The devil take the little bitch!" Bert growled. "I say throw 'er down the stairs and break 'er neck. She be no good to us."

"No, lad. 'Twould be a pity, and we'd collect little ransom for a corpse," Alf said, tightening his hold on his unconscious burden.

"You're a fool, Alf," Jenny said sharply. "Let you see a pretty face and there's milk instead of blood splashing around in your damned veins."

"Enough!" Bert snapped. "Let us be gone, we're wastin' time. The others in the castle may soon be upon us." He started down the stairs, only to be threatened by the duelists again, but Jenny, as before, calmly walked through them. After a second, her companions followed her lead, grinning as those mighty swords fell futilely upon them.

Jenny muttered, "We might have some trouble from the rest o' them. That Sir Francis . . . Remember there are two of them, one living and one dead, but as like to each other as two peas in a pod. The dead one will be clad in garments the like of which you've never seen, and the other wears naught but leather clothes. It'll be him we must needs subdue. If he shows himself, shoot him."

"I don't like these damned ghosts," Bert muttered.

"They can't hurt you," said Jenny scornfully, "unless they throw a scare into you like what happened to poor Pudge. But he always had bone instead of brains in his head."

"Do not speak of 'im like that," Bert muttered. " 'E were a good man."

"Good for nothing," Jenny hissed.

"I'd like to—" Bert began.

"Hush," Alf whispered. "I say we leave the rest o' the swag. This'll be enough." He touched the treasure chest Bert carried. "Those there pearls alone'd bring us thousands o' pounds. Millions, maybe. It be damned 'eavy." He turned to Jenny. "Let's be out 'n' away."

"Not yet," she snarled. "I tell you, there's silver and—"

"It cannot be more'n we 'ave now. And we'll 'old this little wench 'ere for ransom 'n' she'll fetch another tidy sum."

Coming to herself, pressed against Alf's malodorous garments, Arabella upbraided herself again for her carelessness. Her jaw was aching intolerably, but listening to the thieves she realized that she could have lost consciousness only very briefly. She forced herself to remain limp in Alf's hard grasp. The while she hoped against hope that Sir Francis was near. He must be, unless he had been subdued already. And where was the first Sir Francis? He could frighten them, if nothing else.

Then, suddenly, her captor gasped. "W-what be that in the moonlight?"

Jenny laughed derisively. "" 'Tis another of them, you fool, the late and lamented Sir Francis. Look at his garments, man. He died over two hundred years ago. If you do not believe me, I shall walk through him as I did the other two lads."

"Hold, what's that smell?" Bert asked.

"Belike it's your own sweat. I've never seen you in such

a pother," Jenny said contemptuously."

"You never 'ad no nose," Bert growled. "I tell you that's no ghost, that's a man. He's wearing his grandfather's togs," he added, terror lending him unexpected intuition.

"Tell me nothing. Lord, you're shaking like a leaf. Give me the chest," Jenny snapped as she grabbed it from Bert, wincing a little at its weight.

" 'Ere, that be too 'eavy for you."

"Let be," she snapped. She ran down the stairs, toward Sir Francis, and crashed into his surprisingly solid form. He clutched her and managed to remain standing, while the chest fell out of her suddenly nerveless grasp. The force of its fall against the floor broke the ancient hinges, scattering its contents to lie glittering in the moonlight.

A cry of shock and terror escaped Jenny, for she had not believed Bert's warning. Her normal quick-wittedness deserted her, but without conscious direction she struggled to wrench herself free from Sir Francis' hold—only to have him strike a blow that sent her to the gem-laden floor.

A moment later, he moved past her and struck Arabella's captor, Alf. With a howl of agony, Alf loosened his grip on Arabella and dropped to the floor, swearing and groaning.

Moving as swiftly as she could away from Alf's fallen form, Arabella stumbled dazedly into Bert. He seized her and held his dagger hard against her throat, growling at the oncoming Sir Francis, "Stay back or I'll spill 'er guts on this 'ere floor."

Apparently deaf to the threats, Sir Francis moved inexorably forward. Arabella felt Bert's hard grip loosen as he dropped the knife to grab his pistol. He aimed quickly at the approaching man.

With a lightning move, Arabella pushed Bert's arm up, and the shot sped harmlessly over Sir Francis's head. In another moment, Sir Francis had reached Bert and struck him down. Then, gently pushing Arabella out of the way, he lifted Bert with ease, carrying him down to lie with the other fallen thieves, and bound them all securely.

There was laughter in the air and, though she heard it, Arabella did not see those whose merriment filled her ears. She saw only the moonlight-illumined face of Sir Francis as he locked both his arms around her and pressed a long kiss on her lips. Then, raising his head, he said, "You are an interfering little wench, to be sure. But, for now, I must thank you for saving my life."

Words rose to her lips, but she could utter none of them, for the world had contracted to the circle of the arms that held her.

$==11==$

"WELL, WELL, WELL," the constable, a tall, grim-faced man in his early forties, said as he looked at the three groaning, cursing individuals who had just been brought out by his men. He turned his gaze toward Sir Francis, who stood beside Arabella in the vast castle courtyard. "These rogues have figured on many a broadsheet, and there be a reward on their heads. You've earned it right enough, Sir Francis."

"I thank you," Sir Francis said. "But I would prefer to leave it with you for the apprehension of other rogues."

The constable's eyes widened. "That is very kind of you, Sir Francis. Be assured we'll use it for that purpose." He smiled grimly at the prisoners.

" 'Twill be transportation to New South Wales for the men, I'm thinking, and for yon little wench too, I'll be bound."

The constable thanked Sir Francis once again for waiving the reward on the foursome, and Sir Francis and Arabella remained in the courtyard while the constable's men ushered their prisoners into the waiting wagon. Also in the wagon was the body of the late Pudge.

"I know you will put it to good use," Sir Francis assured the constable one last time, as the little cavalcade prepared to depart the castle courtyard.

After they had gone, he turned to Arabella. He smiled as he commented, "A fine night's work."

"Indeed," she said, smiling back. "You were so very brave."

He gave her a long look. "I cannot approve your disobeying of orders meant only for your protection, but neither can I disapprove of your saving my life."

She flushed. "I am very glad I was there to do it, but more credit should go to . . . our ancestors, I think."

"Yes. I could have done nothing were it not for them," he agreed humbly.

"I do not know if that is entirely true, but, still, you cannot think of exorcising them now, I hope."

"Of course I shall not. I will send a message to Dr. Winterbourne this very day."

"Oh, very good. They—" Arabella paused as Ellen, Lady Knollys's elderly abigail, hurried toward them.

"If you please," she said breathlessly. " 'Er ladyship's in a rare takin', and says she must see you at once—both of you—if 'tis possible."

"Of course," Sir Francis assured her, exchanging a questioning look with Arabella, who shrugged. "We will come at once."

"What can she want?" Arabella asked as they followed the abigail back into the castle.

"I imagine she wishes to question us about the events of last night. Probably one or another of the servants has given her an inkling of what took place."

"Where are the jewels now?" Arabella asked nervously.

"I shut them in my strongbox. It is a large one, and they filled it quite. I must, however, present them to my grandmother. They belong to her, by rights."

"Indeed, you must. Why not do it now?" Arabella said.

"Ah, I shall. They are in my chamber. I'll tell Ellen we'll be along shortly." He strode forward and murmured a few words to the woman. At first she appeared very anxious, and though Arabella could not hear the low-voiced exchange that followed, when it ended she saw the woman looked much relieved.

The abigail nodded several times and finished by saying, "I beg you will not be long, sir."

"I promise I shall not," he said, smiling. "It will be a matter of ten minutes at the most."

As the abigail hurried away, Sir Francis said, "Fortunately, my chamber's no great distance from here." He indicated the stairs leading to the first and second floors.

They went up, and Arabella walked with him down the hall. In a short time, they had turned a corner and arrived at a massive portal, which yielded easily to his key.

"If you will do me the kindness of waiting here," he said, "I will fetch our trove."

"Please," Arabella said, flushing slightly as she realized she had been standing very close to him and primed to enter his chamber. An image of Lady Margaret's disapproving face rose and fell before her inner vision, making her doubly or even triply glad that her aunt was in Scotland. Even the fact that, at his request, she had remained in the hall would not have spared her a scolding!

These thoughts fled as Sir Francis returned, carrying a chest a little larger than that which had originally contained the jewels. Taking a fine-gold chain and small key from around his neck, he thrust it into a matching lock and turned it. Then, he pushed back the lid and smiled.

"Oh," Arabella breathed as she stared down at the mass of pearls, emeralds, rubies, sapphires and diamonds—the pearls mostly strung on silken threads, though many were still loose, the gems mounted in massive antique settings, or still unset.

In the sunlight from a nearby window, their bright hues proved dazzling—yet somehow repellent. To see them was to realize that some must have been the belongings of Lady Blanche and her ill-fated young husband. No one knew what other agonies might have been suffered in their procuring.

"I beg you will close the lid," Arabella said. "I wish to see no more."

Sir Francis gave her a long and most understanding look. "We ourselves might have perished for them last night. I will be glad to leave them at my grandmother's disposal." Closing the chest, he put it under his arm. "Come," he said. "It is time and past we obeyed her summons."

They soon arrived at Lady Knollys's suite of rooms and, upon entering, came to a startled stop just beyond the threshold. Her ladyship was smiling up at a shadowy Constance, clinging to the arm of the ghostly Sir Francis. However, that smile vanished immediately her great-grandson and great-niece arrived.

"Good morning, Grandmother," Sir Francis said, smiling. "I bring a treasure to lay at your feet." He set down the chest and pulled its cover back.

She did not give it so much as a glance. "Yes, I had heard it had been recovered. But I must tell you that my pleasure in this . . . acquisition has been spoiled by the . . . the untoward barbarism I understand you contemplate! I know that I am old, but I still retain *all* my senses and, as the head of the family, I must insist on being informed of plans that affect the household!"

"Plans?" Sir Francis regarded her in surprise. "I cannot imagine what you might mean, Grandmother."

"I speak," she said icily, "of the pending visit of this exorcist who, I understand, is to be employed in the routing of my dear, dear relatives, all of whom I regard most highly and love very, very deeply, and have done so since I first encountered them close on eighty years ago! How could you have arranged to employ this . . . this man, without my permission? I am hard put to comprehend so flagrant a breach of family etiquette." Lady Knollys's faded blue eyes actually flashed fire.

"Oh, Aunt, but we are not! We are agreed on that," Arabella cried. "After the great help given us last night, we could never do such a thing. Actually, I was never in favor of it, myself." She flashed an apologetic look at Sir Francis.

He cleared his throat. "Though I did contemplate such an action, and did speak to Dr. Winterbourne, the exorcist from Richmond, I changed my mind on that subject last night. I beg you to believe me, Grandmother, and accept my apologies for distressing you."

There was still fire in her eyes. "And you will send him packing?" she demanded.

"I have every intention of so doing, Grandmother," Sir Francis said with a humility that surprised Arabella.

Lady Knollys expelled a long breath. Then, in less acerbic tones, she said, "I hold myself partially accountable for this contretemps. I expect I should have discussed our apparitions with you more thoroughly." She sighed. "I am so used to their presences that I forget that, to newcomers, they present rather a surprise. You, Francis, will eventually inherit this castle. May I hope that you will not put this nefarious plan into action immediately I am gone?"

"I promise you that I will not," he said quickly. "As I have explained, I have strong reasons to be extremely grateful to them—especially to Sir Francis, my distant uncle."

"I am not as distant as you imagine, my dear nephew," Sir Francis said, moving forward, his arms still around the waist of Constance. "As you see." He smiled.

"I did not mean distant in the way of proximity. I meant—" Sir Francis began.

Constance laughed. "We know what you meant, Sir Francis."

"Oh," Arabella breathed. "It is lovely to see you again, Constance. How—er—do you feel?"

Constance smiled. "In common with Hamlet, I was rather frightened about shuffling off my so-called mortal coil, but I feel ever so much better now that my cough has ceased to trouble me. And I am finally with the man I have loved for so very long a time." She directed a glowing look at Sir Francis and received an extremely tender smile from him. "But," she continued, "I do hope my, er, mortal remains will not be sent to my home. I would rather they were buried in the family graveyard— if that is not too bold a request?"

"Your mortal remains shall lie beside mine, my dearest love," the first Sir Francis said, his gaze shifting from Constance to rest compellingly on his nephew's face.

"I will see to the arranging of that, my dears," Lady Knollys said firmly. "I am not yet in my dotage. Francis will transmit my orders to the appropriate people."

"Indeed, I shall," Sir Francis agreed. "In fact, I am in complete accord with Constance."

"As am I," Arabella said warmly. "She belongs here, and—" She paused at a knock on the door.

"Please come in," Lady Knollys called.

George, one of the footmen, opened the door. "If you please, milady, Doctor Winterbourne has arrived."

"Doctor Winterbourne?" she questioned.

"The—er—exorcist, grandmother," Sir Francis said, reddening.

"Oh, dear," said Constance, drawing nearer to Sir Francis I, who flung a protective arm around her shoulders, the while he gazed sternly at his nephew.

"Show him into the drawing room," Sir Francis instructed, "and tell him we will be with him directly." As the servant left, he turned to Lady Knollys. "I beg you will not be concerned, Grandmother—nor either of you," his gaze took in Constance and his many-times-removed uncle. "I have given my word that he will be dismissed, and I shall attend to that immediately."

"I will hold you to that word, Francis," Lady Knollys said sternly.

"You need not worry," Arabella said gently.

"Come, my dear," Sir Francis said briskly, "let us rout the ghost-hunter."

"I wish you had not to see him at all," Arabella said as they came down the stairs. "He is sure to be extremely disappointed."

"Yes," he agreed ruefully, "but I could hardly send him away without a word. Richmond is some distance from here. I shall have to give him something for his pains."

"Yes," she agreed quickly. "I had not thought of that. But what will you say to him?"

"The truth, my dearest."

The words he had spoken just now, the new tenderness in his voice, the warmth of his smile, activated a whole series of pulses throughout Arabella's body.

There had been no declaration as yet, but unless she

were deeply mistaken, one would be forthcoming, and soon. Arabella's pleasant thoughts were abruptly scattered as, on entering the drawing room, she saw a tall, pontifical-appearing gentleman seated on the sofa. He rose immediately as she and Sir Francis entered, and Arabella, continuing her clerical comparison, decided that he looked not unlike the incumbent of St. James's, her parish church—an unctuous gentleman she could not abide!

Dr. Winterbourne had a large portmanteau beside his chair that, at first glance, suggested that he had come to stay the night. Arabella decided, however, that if this were true, the butler would have appropriated the portmanteau so as to have it taken to the chamber allotted to the gentleman.

"Ah, good morning, Doctor Winterbourne," Sir Francis said cordially.

A little too cordially, Arabella decided, guessing that her cousin was embarrassed by the change of mind and heart that would let the ghosts remain and speed the exorcist on his way.

"Good morning, sir."

Dr. Winterbourne raised his head. Like a hound scenting a kill was the unfortunate analogy that occurred to Arabella.

Before Sir Francis could respond to his salutation, the exorcist added, "Yes, yes, yes, I feel them. . . . Five you said, I believe. Yes, there are five, and full of animosity, too. That is not surprising. In the last house I visited there were more, and their displeasure was quite as palpable as that which I am currently encountering. They will need to be sent away, and quickly. They are all very dangerous and have remained here far, far, too long. Yes, a very long time, else I would not be experiencing their combined animosity so strongly."

His mellifluous tones reminded Arabella even more strongly of that same cleric who had earlier figured in her mind's eye. She hastily swallowed the laughter that threatened, as Sir Francis, evidently priming himself to break the bad news to the good doctor, said with a cordiality that she was sure was assumed, "Will you not sit down, Doctor Winterbourne? There is much I must tell you."

"Ah, Sir Francis, you need not tell me as much as you imagine. I see them. They are of the opinion, of course, that their invisibility protects them—but I, who have been dealing with revenants these thirty-odd years, know all about their shifts and tricks. They, of course, do not wish to leave this so-called vale of tears for the dark shores to which they, by their various crimes, are naturally bound."

"Oh, dear," Arabella murmured.

The doctor bent a surprised look upon her. "You appear distressed—er—Madame."

"You must pardon me, sir!" Sir Francis exclaimed. "I have neglected to introduce you to my cousin, Lady Arabella Arden."

"I am delighted to make your acquaintance, your ladyship," Dr. Winterbourne said, bestowing a brief smile upon her. Then, before she could respond, he continued in smooth and, she thought, unctuous tones. "I do understand your feeling. It is not easy to dwell in a house plagued by evil spirits, particularly those who boldly put themselves forward."

"I do not believe they are precisely evil," Sir Francis said quickly.

He received an astonished look from the exorcist. "You—do—not—condone—a woman who slew her husband and three small children and—and another female who was flagrantly unfaithful to her husband with her brother-in-law, who also haunts this castle? And what about the two young rogues who followed the banner of Richard I to the Holy Land?"

Arabella protested, "Anything they may have done was in battle, and they themselves were slain before they really had time to live."

"Ah, you are a romantic young lady, I see, but not

every man who took the cross could be described as saintly, Lady Arabella."

"I am sure my cousin is quite aware of that," Sir Francis said sternly.

"Yes, I am sure she is, and has only gilded the past with present romance. Now, as to my methods of dispatching these five entities, my senses tell me that I must needs employ the additional services of a colleague, a clergyman, who is wise in the ways of specters and, with me, will employ bell, book, and candle to rout them. We have worked together on many of my more difficult assignments, which, I feel, this one promises to be. He is currently employed in ridding the church of a nearby parish of a ghostly coven."

He shook his head, adding in pained accents, "Imagine, the effrontery of those revenants—to invade a church! No matter, they will soon receive their comeuppance from him—because there are none of the ghostly persuasion who can withstand the awesome power of bell, book, and candle. I wish he were free now—for the sooner we begin, the better it will be." Unlocking his portmanteau, he reached inside, producing a battered Bible.

"This—" he began, and then uttered a cry as the volume suddenly flew from his hand. He paled. "There is a most dangerous entity h-here."

As if in answer to that statement, the chandelier, which Arabella noticed for the first time was much like that in the dining room, swayed back and forth, its crystal ornaments clashing together.

It's rather musical, Arabella thought as she exchanged a hasty glance with Sir Francis just as the chandelier ceased its motion and the drops became still.

"Ah, as usual, the Latin has proved effective," Dr. Winterbourne said, bringing out a large handkerchief and wiping his brow.

"The Latin?" Arabella inquired.

"I spoke it under my breath—Church Latin, to be exact," Dr. Winterbourne explained. "We should begin the exorcism even sooner than I imagined."

"Where would they go once they left here?" Arabella asked nervously, though she knew her cousin would never let this horrid man have his way.

"Why, to the lower regions, which they have eluded all these years, my dear young lady," Dr. Winterbourne explained with considerable satisfaction.

"Have they actually *eluded* hell?" Sir Francis asked. "I am reminded of Christopher Marlowe's *Dr. Faustus*. It was his Mephistopheles who said of Earth, 'Why this is hell nor am I out of it . . . Thinkst thou that I, who saw the face of God and tasted the eternal joys of heaven, am not tormented with ten thousand hells in being deprived of eternal bliss.' "

"A play, only," Dr. Winterbourne said, smiling deprecatingly.

"In my estimation, the lines ring true," Sir Francis commented.

"Yes," Arabella breathed, "especially now." She added, "How effective are the—er—bell, book, and candle? And do you have them with you?"

"Indeed, I have. I always carry them with me," Dr. Winterbourne assured her. "You have seen my Bible. Here," he reached into his portmanteau, "is the bell." He brought out a large bell that to Arabella's mind much resembled a cowbell. He gave it a little shake, and it produced a clang. In that same moment other clangs were heard—louder and seemingly issuing from all corners of the chamber while, above, the chandelier shook once more.

"Good God, what's that?" The exorcist had paled, but Sir Francis smiled genially.

"I imagine it is our five entities signaling that they would as lief not be exorcised."

"Not five," Arabella reminded Sir Francis, "six. You must not forget Constance."

"Oh, yes, I was forgetting," he said rather ruefully. "Six, then. I am sure Constance does not wish to be exorcised either." He turned to Dr. Winterbourne. "I have brought you here under what must seem like false pretenses. I have changed my mind. I do not wish this exorcism to proceed."

The doctor was trembling. "B-but, it must proceed. T-t-they m-must be exorcised!" he actually bleated. "I . . . I n-never h-heard the . . . the like."

"And you with so many successful exorcisms to your credit, Dr. Winterbourne?" Sir Francis said with a fine edge of sarcasm to his tones.

"I . . . I m-m-must prepare m-myself ere I . . . I c-can d-deal with them. . . . P-p-preparation is . . . n-n-needed." He rose, his face white and his hands trembling. "I . . . I t-think I . . . I m-must g-g-go!"

"I will see you to the door and tell the man to have your horse brought round, Doctor Winterbourne. And there is no need for you to return. I will, of course, make sure you are appropriately reimbursed," Sir Francis said equably, not looking at Arabella.

She was very pleased. Had he exchanged so much as a side glance with her, she was quite sure, she would have been totally unable to quell her burgeoning laughter.

Once at the front door, Sir Francis, having delivered his orders to the butler, his expression still carefully noncommittal, handed the large case to the trembling Dr. Winterbourne. There was a sudden stiff breeze that made the portmanteau sway, and the doctor stumbled, scattering his paraphernalia over the floor of the chamber.

"Oh, Doctor Winterbourne!" Sir Francis said, concerned, "I am very sorry. The—er—entities are in a rather playful mood this morning. Here, let me help you retrieve your . . . tools."

"The devil fly away with you," the doctor bellowed, glaring at Sir Francis furiously as he futilely scrambled for his tools and papers, only to have the lightest of them roll and flutter out of reach each time he neared them.

In the midst of this confusion, the butler returned to announce that the doctor's horse had been brought round.

"I think we should have the stablehand assist this gentleman into his saddle," Sir Francis advised.

Having grabbed as much of his paraphernalia as he could find and thrust it into his case, the exorcist stuttered, "There . . . is n-no need. Once I . . . I am out of h-here . . ." He rushed out the front door with Sir Francis following and Arabella coming to stand just beyond that same door.

As he approached his mount, a roan mare, she gave a terrified neigh, and reared, nearly escaping the stablehand's grasp. The doctor rushed to mount as soon as the horse was still again, scrambling into his saddle at the same time that the mare, with another distraught neigh, broke free of the stablehand's control and galloped off with her rider desperately clinging to her mane, the reins having fallen from his palsied grasp.

"By all that's holy!" gasped the butler.

"I think," Sir Francis remarked with admirable sangfroid, "that I must disagree with you there, James." Without elaborating upon that comment, he went inside.

Just beyond the door, he found Arabella, trembling. Tears were coursing down her cheeks.

"My dearest," he cried, concerned, "What is amiss?" He led her into the drawing room and indicated a large padded chair.

She sank into it gratefully, but it was a minute before she could reply. " 'T-'tis n-nothing. I . . . I watched him leave . . . that's all. I . . . I know it is wrong to l-laugh at the poor man, but . . . but . . ." More laughter escaped her.

"It is not wrong, love," he assured her quickly. "It would have been wrong only if you had not laughed at that sententious charlatan. Thank the powers that be, you are not of a nature to suffer fools gladly.

"Indeed, my dearest Arabella—" He broke off as the butler appeared again, carrying a tray on which reposed a letter. "Yes, James?" he inquired.

"This just came for you, sir. 'Twas brought by messenger. The man who delivered it said as how 'tis important and he be waitin' for an answer."

"Have him sit in the hall. I'll be there directly," Sir Francis instructed. Looking at the envelope, he frowned.

"By God, this is from Jean. I know his writing." He turned to Arabella. "I pray you will excuse me while I read this—it might be important."

"Of course," she said, feeling an odd pounding in her throat.

Extracting a long sheet of thin paper, he read it slowly, his frown deepening. Subsequently, an audible sigh escaped him, confirming Arabella's fear that the missive contained disturbing news—something, she realized, she had felt when the butler had first produced the letter. It was with difficulty that she restrained herself from inquiring as to its contents. If he wished her to know, he would tell her.

Finally, he looked up. "I must leave within the hour," he said abruptly. "I am to go with the messenger who brought this letter. Jean, my valet, who has never been in France, but who has several relatives there, has unaccountably been mistaken for an escaped felon. He lies in prison and is in danger of execution."

"Good gracious," Arabella cried. "Oh, dear, the poor man. Of course you must go. I only pray that—that you will not be putting yourself in danger, too."

"I am sure I shall not; I can easily prove Jean's identity. I am most loath to go, but you see—Jean is not just my valet, he is also my foster brother."

"You have no choice," Arabella said. "It is a long ride to Dover, I fear. It must be over two hundred miles."

"Yes, it is nearer three hundred. . . ." He moved to her. "May I hope you will be here when I return?"

"I will. Of course I will. Oh, dear, where has my mind gone. My father is in Paris—I can give you his direction. He is on a diplomatic mission and can, perhaps, help you. Oh, where are pen and paper—in the library, of course. I will go at once," she said distractedly.

"That would be helpful," he said gratefully. "Oh, my dear, I do wish—but, no matter, I must go. And again, please, be here when I return."

"I promise I shall," she said.

In another moment, he had hurried to his chamber and

she to the library to scrawl out her father's direction. As she sat at the desk, the tears that had been threatening rolled down her cheeks, but she wiped them away hastily.

She wished she could as easily wipe away her burgeoning fears, but she could not. Still, to worry over Sir Francis's journey to Paris, and his confrontation with authorities who might still be filled with impotent anger over the second banishment of Napoleon Bonaparte and looking for trouble, would do her little good. She would have to hope for the best, pray for the best, and present a smiling face to Sir Francis when he left the castle.

=12=

HE HAD BEEN gone for only three days, a mere seventy-two hours, but desolation, like a dark cloud come from nowhere to block out the sun, settled on Arabella. She had promised to wait for Sir Francis. How long would that wait last?

The ghosts spoke comforting words—promising a safe return. She was grateful to them, but felt that their predictions should not be allowed to carry much weight. They were only paying lip service to her situation, concerned as they were with themselves. Even Constance, immersed in the new aspect of her relationship with her own Sir Francis, uttered what Arabella considered mere platitudes concerning that happy future awaiting her.

Once or twice she had sought Lady Knollys's chamber, but invariably, her aged aunt was deep in conversation with one or another entity on the subject of the transition, which, of course, was most interesting to one who had lived so very long.

Now, as Arabella lay abed long past her usual rising time, she wished— But it was useless to wish for some manner of communication from him, who was riding to Dover, his mind intent on his foster brother's plight!

Consequently, when she could bring herself to rise, she would go down to the library, where, amongst the heavy tomes dealing with history, most of it ancient, there were to be found effusions by Aphra Behn, Tobias Smollett, and Jonathan Swift.

Naturally, there was nothing from the Minerva Press, and though she had tried to read the books she had brought with her, she did not find them nearly as exciting or engrossing as she had anticipated. Even those tales that were replete with ghosts rang false after her encounters with bona fide specters.

She had gone riding twice but, on each occasion, she had envisioned Sir Francis at her side and, on returning, she worried more about his journey to Dover, hoping that he was safe.

And what would take place once he reached Paris? Given the volatile temper of the French, might not he, too, run into trouble? It was even possible that he could be imprisoned as well!

It seemed amazing that he had been gone only three days. It felt as if so many weeks had passed and when . . . when . . . when would he come riding back? And, suppose he did not. Suppose . . . These melancholy conjectures ended abruptly as Ann, the girl who had been acting as her abigail, hurried into her chamber.

"Oh, milady," she said nervously. "The lady be 'ere and says as 'ow you must be dressed, for she's comin' to see you!"

Arabella regarded her confusedly. "Who, pray, is here?"

"I am," Lady Margaret said, stalking into Arabella's chamber. "It is unusual for you to lie abed so long. It's close on ten o' clock!"

"Aunt Margaret!" Arabella regarded her incredulously. "I—I thought you were in Scotland."

"And so I have been, and am on my way home. Did you not receive my letter?"

"No," Arabella said.

"Oh, Lord, I am not surprised. Everything in this part of the world is at sixes and sevens. Your father, my love, has returned from France. But I suppose you are aware of that, at least."

"N-no," Arabella said, thinking that her father's direction would now be of little use to Sir Francis, since he was no longer in Paris.

"Has your father not written?" Lady Margaret demanded.

"No," Arabella said, and sighed. "But I expect he's not had the time for it if, indeed, he is still there."

Her aunt regarded her blankly. "I am not sure I understand you, my dear."

"If he is still in Paris," Arabella said.

"I have just explained that he is no longer in Paris. He is in London. Have you gone daft, my dear?"

"Oh." Arabella sighed again. "I . . . I was thinking of something else."

"Obviously," Lady Margaret commented sharply. "Well, no matter, I have come to take you home. Your father is most anxious to see you."

"But I did not expect he would be home so soon."

"No more did I, but he writes that he is quite out of sympathy with the French court, which seems sunk in apathy, even though there are so many English there. Oh, well, I shall not refine upon his state of mind. Certainly, he will paint a vivid picture of it upon our return."

"Our return!" Arabella cried. "But—but I cannot leave here."

"You cannot leave," her aunt echoed. "Nonsense!"

"No," Arabella protested. "I have promised to wait for . . . someone."

"And who might this someone be?" Lady Margaret demanded frigidly.

Belatedly recalling that her aunt had met him, Arabella said, "Sir Francis. You have met him."

"Oh, yes, a well-spoken young man, if rather peculiarly clad."

"His valet was detained in Paris."

"This discussion is far from the point. You must come home with me, Arabella. Your father has sent for you, and I cannot imagine your wanting to remain in this castle. Indeed, every time I have remembered that horrid shaking, I have had sleepless nights praying you were safe. Thank God you are, but let us not tempt fate any further, for—" She broke off, as overhead the crystal

157

drops of the small chandelier in Arabella's bedchamber clashed together.

With a cry, Arabella's aunt scrambled to her feet. "It's at it again!" she gasped. "Have . . . your abigail p-pack for you. We—we leave within the hour."

"No, please," Arabella protested. "I must stay."

"You must not. Pack what you need and let us go!"

Vainly, an anguished Arabella pleaded, citing the hoped-for return of Sir Francis, to which her aunt said pointedly, "And has this young man offered?"

"He—he has suggested. I mean, I am certain he was about to do so, but the—the message from his valet came and—"

"A man who prefers his valet to you is not the sort you should encourage, my love," Lady Margaret said sharply. "And, fortunately, you are not of an age to make this decision. We will leave, as I have said, as near immediately as possible."

Dolefully sitting in the well-sprung coach bearing her from the castle, Arabella leaned out the window, her tears caught by the breeze. Her misery was manifest. What would Sir Francis think? She had left a note for him with Lady Knollys, and she prayed her elderly aunt would remember to give it to him.

If only Constance had remained alive, she would have seen to it that he received it, but Arabella could not regret Constance's demise. She was so much happier now. And to do Constance's Sir Francis credit, beyond a few polite words of regret at her hasty departure, he had not spoken to her. Indeed, since Constance had joined him, he had not made the slightest effort to flirt with anyone.

The words "reformed rake," had darted through her mind and he, smiling at her, had said, " 'Tis the truth, my dear, and how could it not be? My Constance, constant to the end, is a miracle. She has given me, she has given us all great happiness. Greater, indeed, than any of us deserve."

"No," Arabella had said. "It is time and past your sins were forgiven."

He had appeared vaguely frightened. "Say not so, my dear. Say, instead, forgot." With an impish gleam in his eyes, he had added, "I cannot imagine that any of us, save Constance, here, would feel comfortable in heaven."

"As far as I am concerned," Constance had said, gazing up at him with her heart in her eyes, "this is heaven."

Tears had rolled down Arabella's cheeks as she watched them move into a long embrace. While she could not envy them, an image of herself and her Sir Francis in that same pose had flickered before her eyes.

What would he think when he returned to the castle and found that she was gone, after having promised to wait for him? He would be disappointed, perhaps even angry.

She had only Constance's parting words to comfort her. "Be not afraid, my dear. All will come to pass as you hope."

But her beloved was in France, a place where so many had met so cruel a fate. Where, under Napoleon, so many young men had ridden off to die in foreign fields. Furthermore, the English were not popular in France, even though her father obviously had not met with difficulties. Still, Louis XVIII had been driven from his throne once. Might it not happen again and . . . But it was futile to speculate. She could only hope for the best.

"An Incomparable!" Clemency cried. "Oh, are you not thrilled, excited, overwhelmed—oh, dear, I have run out of words." She gazed at Arabella in surprise. "*You* do not appear to be in the least excited," she said in accusatory tones.

"Oh, I expect it is a great honor," Arabella said.

"You 'expect it is a great honor,' " Clemency echoed. "The Bow Window Set at White's has judged you an Incomparable. Even though poor Beau Brummell is off to Calais, that is still considered—" she was adding sarcastically.

159

"Oh, I know," Arabella interrupted. "And, of course, I am grateful." She sighed.

" 'Patience upon a monument,' " Clemency commented.

"And what, pray, is that supposed to suggest?" Arabella demanded.

" 'She never told her love . . .' Oh, you know, Viola in *Twelfth Night* . . . 'she never told her love but let concealment, like a worm in the bud, feed on her damask cheek.' And she also sat 'like patience upon a monument.' Something, my dear, is feeding on your damask cheek. I do hope it is not a worm."

"Oh, you do speak such nonsense!" Arabella snapped.

"Nonsense, is it? I happen to know that you have received three proposals since you returned from that castle—and have refused them all. Lord Houghton spoke of putting a period to his existence."

"And the very next week was seen with Lady Cornelia Satterleigh, waltzing at Almack's," Arabella reminded her.

"Well, that is tantamount to putting an end to his existence, if he offers for her. Such a bore as that creature is."

"Is she?"

"Entirely, but you *know* that. I vow, Arabella, your mind seems wandering on some inland sea. Is that not poetic? I just thought of it. To change the subject, have you read *The Haunted Castle* by A Lady, she calls herself. It is most— Gracious Arabella, what have I said to make you weep?"

"N-nothing, C-Clemency, oh, dear, I am sorry, I feel— I—I mean I am not really myself." Arabella put a handkerchief to her streaming eyes. "I—I must—I mean *you* must excuse me."

"Oh, I shall, of course," Clemency said, putting her arms around Arabella and kissing her on the cheek. "I do hope you'll soon be feeling more the thing."

Having bidden a moist farewell to Clemency, Arabella repaired to the library, where she began to weep in earnest. Why hadn't she told Clemency that it was she who had written *The Haunted Castle*—dashed it off in the first weeks of her return. Developing the plot in her mind during the wearisome hours of the return trip was the only thing that had saved her sanity. But now it was written and selling in the bookshops, and she had nothing to direct her mind and save her from pursuing the same thoughts around and around, over and over again. It had been fully eight weeks since she had left the castle, and it was now close on September. Autumn was nearly upon them and, as far as Arabella's mood was concerned, she might as well have been existing in the depths of winter.

Surely, Sir Francis must have returned from France by now. Had he received her note? She had left it with Lady Knollys; had she forgotten to give it to him? Had he forgotten her? Had he met a charming French girl? Rumor had it that there were a great number of these at the court of Louis XVIII.

"Eight weeks . . ." Arabella moaned. Earlier calculations had given her the melancholy sum of thirteen hundred and forty-four hours as the amount of time that had passed since last she had seen him. If one went by minutes . . . But she was being ridiculous.

"Ah, here you are, Arabella," Lord Dartmoor said as he came into the library. He was smiling.

In fact, he seemed extremely pleased about something, his daughter thought, envying him. "Pleasure" was currently lacking from her vocabulary.

"You seem in an excellent mood, Papa," she commented, wanting to know the source of that particular mood, even if she could not share in it.

"I am." His smile broadened. "A certain young man of an excellent family has offered for your hand and—"

"No, no, and no," Arabella cried. "I am not interested! I do not want to marry!"

"My dear," he protested, "will you not hear me out?"

He had not ordered her to heed him. He had put it in the form of a request. For this consideration of her feelings she must be grateful, if not receptive. She said, albeit grudgingly, "Pray continue, Papa."

He was silent a moment, staring at her worriedly. "I am sorry," he said finally, "that you have developed this strange antipathy to all thought of marriage. You cannot wish to remain unwed. Think of your aunt Margaret. She was much in demand as a young woman and, since our father would not press her to accept any of the gentlemen who offered for her hand, she continued single. And then, upon reaching the age of twenty-four, she grew desperate and married the next man who proposed to her—an impecunious youth who got himself killed in a duel soon after they were married, leaving her with the daughter, whom she cherished most tenderly, only to have the girl marry a Scotsman and leave for Edinburgh. The only time she is in communication with her beloved Rosalie is when the poor girl is about to have another child. She has, I might mention, five children—but you know that, I presume."

"I do," Arabella said. "Even though I had no inkling of her history." She sighed. "Oh, dear, I am sorry."

"I beg you will not reveal any knowledge of her . . . unfortunate past."

"Oh, I never, never shall," Arabella cried. "I promise you that, Papa."

"I thank you. And since I do not want you to remain in single-blessedness, or make a mean marriage like your poor aunt, please do me the favor of seeing this young man, my love."

He looked so concerned that Arabella found she had not the heart to refuse him. "Very well, Papa. I will see him." She loosed a long sigh. "But, beyond that . . ."

"We'll not speak of 'beyond that,' my dear. I will be satisfied just to have you meet him."

Once he had quitted the library, Arabella, sinking down in a chair, buried her face in her hands and gave way to the tears she had had difficulty in restraining all through that most unfortunate conversation.

She had longed to tell her father about Sir Francis, but

pride had silenced her and, furthermore, what good would it have done to speak about someone with whom she had enjoyed such a brief acquaintance, if one went by days. However, once this suitor arrived, she would gently but firmly discourage him—and as soon as she might.

"Oh, milady, if you do not look a picture!" Meg exclaimed as Arabella, clad in one of the gowns her father had brought her from Paris, rose from her dressing table. "Thank you, Meg. I have always been partial to this shade of green."

She glanced into the full-length tilt mirror, which stood in its handsome mahogany frame in one corner. Meg was right. She was, indeed, looking well. The gown in her favorite Pomona green was simple in cut, but immensely flattering both to her fair coloring and to her green eyes. Meg had taken especial pains with her hair—some of which escaped from her braids to curl most fetchingly about her face. She was also wearing a pair of long filigree earrings, set with tiny cameos to match her cameo necklace, also a present from her father.

He did have excellent taste, she thought, and hoped that in the long years of her maidenhood, he would not regret the amount of money he had lavished upon her wardrobe.

She did have a moment of sympathy for her unknown suitor. No doubt, given her appearance and her large dowry, he would be much cast down at her chill reception of his offer. Furthermore, she would not keep him dangling in suspense. She would tell him right out that she would never marry unless . . . But she would not even consider the "unless"!

She had not heard from *him*, and pride had kept her from writing to her Aunt Juliana—even though she was sure that Sir Francis must have communicated with her. Or had he collected his valet and gone back to Canada?

The delicate chime of the clock on her mantelpiece announcing the hour of seven, the time when her caller was expected, caused her to tense. A second later, she moved slowly to the door and, once in the hall, walked slowly to the head of the stairs and came slowly down them.

On entering the drawing room, she cast a quick glance about her. Much to her relief, he had not yet arrived. Only her father was present, and he was rising from his chair.

"Ah, my love, you certainly make a beautiful picture," he said warmly. "That gown matches your eyes to perfection, as I thought it must when I saw the silk in a Parisian boutique."

"I do thank you, Papa," she said, "and must needs thank you a second time for having it made. It fits me extremely well."

"Does it not?" Lady Margaret said, entering on that comment. She surveyed Arabella with considerable approval. "Indeed, my child, I have never seen you in such looks. Have you, Edward?"

"No, I must agree with you, Margaret, dear."

"I do thank you," Arabella said, wondering nervously what they would think when they viewed her cool reception of her prospective and unwanted suitor. Indeed, thinking of their subsequent comments, she was reminded of—

But in that moment all thoughts fled as the butler appeared and announced, "Sir Francis Knollys, your lordship."

Arabella, her eyes widening, stood perfectly still as a tall, handsome young man was ushered into the chamber. Her first wild thought was that it could not be he. It had to be another of the same name—this stylishly garbed gentleman, with short dark locks curling around his face in a way reminding her of the bust of a Roman soldier she had seen in the British Museum. However, it was indeed *he*.

With a little cry of joy, she dashed across the room to be clasped in Sir Francis's arms and passionately embraced.

"Oh," she cried when finally he released her. "You— you've found your valet."

"Indeed, I have, and more to the point, I have found you," he said warmly.

"I—I know I was not there to receive you, but you—you see—" she began.

"I see, and I know what happened. And—" He flushed as Lord Dartmoor came to his side.

"Oh, Papa," Arabella said hastily. "It is Sir Francis, you see."

"I do see," Lord Dartmoor said, smiling. "And I also see that you spoke no more than the truth, Sir Francis. Needless to say, I am delighted at your reading of the situation. My daughter's adamant refusals to the many offers she has recently received had me quite worried—but I must assure you, I could not be more pleased at her choice. You also, I believe, will find you have made a happy choice. Nobody could have made me happier than her dear mother.

"How fortunate," he continued with a little smile, "that you are only *third* cousins. I might have had something to say if you had been first or second cousins, but nobody can say a third cousinship is anything except respectable. You have my unstinted approval."

"I thank you, sir," Sir Francis said rather huskily. He looked as if he longed to embrace Arabella again, but contented himself with slipping an arm around her waist as he added, "I am in hopes that the wedding may take place soon."

"Tomorrow!" Arabella cried.

"No," Lady Margaret protested. "There is the church to be secured, and banns to be read, and—"

"Nonsense, Margaret," Lord Dartmoor interrupted. "Let it be as soon as they wish."

"Now!" Arabella cried.

"Next week, I think," Lord Dartmoor said smiling. "We will have to obtain a special license and find some member of the clergy to perform the ceremony. Will that be sufficiently soon, young man?"

He glanced in the direction of his prospective son-in-law. Then, moving toward Lady Margaret's chair, he

took her hand and pointed to the door. She smiled, nodded and, rose to follow him from the chamber.

Neither Arabella nor Sir Francis was aware of that
tactful departure. Caught in another long embrace, they
had eyes and lips only for each other.

If you would like to receive details about other Walker Regency Romances, please write to:

The Regency Editor
Walker and Company
720 Fifth Avenue
New York, New York 10019